I0579908

On The Couch

A Dog's Tale

David Johnson & Morgan Voorhis

Shoofly
Books

Shoofly Books
An Imprint of HBE Publishing

All inquiries should be addressed to: couchadogstale@gmail.com
HBE Publishing
640 Clovis Ave
Clovis, CA, 93612
http://www.hbepublishing.com

ISBN 978-1-943050-47-5 TRADE PAPERBACK
ISBN 978-1-943050-48-2 EBOOK

Printed in the United States of America
December 2016

Dedication

This book is dedicated to our beloved dog, Nagi, an abandoned pound rescue, who was with us for a short nine years before succumbing to bone cancer.

We further dedicate this book to the millions of animals who, like Nagi, are abandoned, neglected and abused.

CHAPTER ONE

RESCUED

Be careful what you wish for. Sometimes it can turn around and bite you in the butt. That's what happened to Caleb and me. Let's just say it seems fitting that our first and last meeting involved prison bars.

It all started the day Caleb took me home to live with him and his wife, Becca. Now, don't get me wrong. I was excited to be rescued (just in the nick of time, I might add) from that pound prison. However, had I known the crazy twists and turns my life would ultimately take, I may have been more prone to tempt fate, keeping my paws crossed that other compassionate parents would find me appealing and take me home.

Nevertheless, my story needs to be told as a cautionary tale for other four-leggers, too quick to jump at the first opportunity for freedom.

Let me take you back a short five years…

Another uneventful day in the pound. It's so boring here. Nothing to chase. Nothing to do. The only thing that keeps me from total insanity is analyzing my recurring dream that spins around and around in my head. What can it possibly mean? The parts I remember are utterly ridiculous and disjointed. In my dream, I'm sprawled across an over-stuffed couch. On the wall are two framed licenses; some kind of certificates. I try to make out the details, but only the words "marriage" on one and "co-therapist" on the other pop out.

Before I have time to make out more of the wording, I'm distracted by clipped, darting movements across the room. What in the world is happening on that desk?

A little black beetle appears, wearing a miniature baseball cap, backwards, and six tiny roller skates. He has somehow fashioned his own private skate ramp using a long yellow pencil, placed on an incline from the desk top to the rim of a coffee cup. This tiny, odd creature zooms down the pencil screaming with delight, then climbs up the chain on the nearby Tiffany-style desk lamp. He swings over to the rim of the coffee cup and down the pencil he goes, again and again. Each time, squealing louder and louder.

The only other thing I remember, is a photograph of a platinum blond with a fluffy, cotton-candy hairdo. Scrawled in barely legible letters across the bottom corner of the photo is the name "Marilyn."

Like I mentioned earlier, my sleeping hours are filled with my dream while my waking hours are filled with fruitlessly analyzing my dream, despite the noisy background of endless whining and barking.

One day, while trying to get in a few much-needed winks, a terrible sense of dread and doom descends upon me. My inner sense tells me that my time is just about up. This stomach-churning foreboding is validated when I overhear a staff conversation in which I only have a few more hours before my jailers "compassionately" put me down. Put me down where? If I have any input, I'd like to be put down in a grassy meadow with hundreds of fat squirrels to chase.

My cellmate corrects my misguided thinking, explaining that "put down" is merely a fancy way of saying I will be given a special last meal before my execution. Execution? I didn't even have a trial with a jury of my peers. I'll admit I was relentless in my pursuit of neighborhood cats ... and in plotting great escapes, which ultimately led my owners to angrily toss me in the car, drive for miles and dump me out in the middle of nowhere. But given these facts, aren't they the ones who committed the crime? So why aren't they locked up before being "put down?" After all, I'm a dog and dogs not only chase cats but can be remarkable escape-artists. It's inherent to our nature.

Anyway, that's how I landed in this prison, but I ask you again, does my punishment fit my so-called crime? Whatever happened to innocent until proven guilty, or does that legal-ease only apply to two-leggers? It makes me wonder if my fellow prisoners have also been dumped, discarded or abandoned. Imprisoned through no fault of their own. The silence becomes deafening. It's almost as though the other captives worry, too.

Suddenly, a welcome distraction grows closer. A two-legger with a low raspy voice strolls by each cage.

"Hi boy, you're a handsome little guy. Wha' cha doing in there?" What does it look like we're doing?

He talks like we're toddlers with mush for brains.

Unexpectedly, he stops in front of my cell. While he sizes me up, I do the same. Eccentric ... know-it-all ... a hugger ... no thanks, I'll pass. We stand foot-to-paw, eye-to-eye, locked in a stare-down contest. He seems more amused by this competition than I am.

Of course, I want out of prison, but not with him. I didn't have a good feeling about him. He just didn't smell right. It's a dog thing, you know. But then, my alternatives are relatively few, so I give him a semi-friendly wag of my tail. He doesn't say a word, just smiles and pats my nose. There's something almost piti-ful about him. Something that compels me to, unchar-acteristically, lick his outstretched hand.

One of the prison guards, noticing a possible connection, suggests that this human take me outside to the courtyard for a "test run." Is it for his benefit or mine? I can already tell you that he won't pass muster.

Before asking my opinion, I'm yanked from my cell and a tattered, worn leash is placed around my neck.

I smell freedom as the heavy metal door swings open. However, before I have set even one paw on the warm grass, I spot the Collie who had kept me awake the night before. Naturally, having a score to settle, I lunge forward, obsessed with my mission to attack this rude beast who dared interrupt my late-night dream. Before I make contact, the human jerks me back so hard, I tumble and lay sprawled at his feet.

The guard, who has observed this interaction, shakes her head commenting: "I have to be honest with you, Sir. This dog really isn't very adoptable. He's older, larger, un-neutered and un-socialized. Why don't you take a look at one of our more adoptable selections?"

The two-legger smirks at her suggestion. "I'm very patient. I have to be in my line of work. Believe me, I'll show this little rascal what's what and who's who in no time. Besides, I do enjoy a challenge. You know ... spice things up a bit."

As good fortune would have it, this human, Caleb, has some odd need to save the lost and damned, so against my better judgment and probably his, we nervously make a silent agreement to co-habitat that day. Neither of us utters a single word on the trip home.

To this day, I can't figure out why he adopted me.

Maybe he was bullied as a kid and no one was there to guide him or stand up for him. Maybe he liked lost causes. Maybe he wanted to get back at Becca, his wife.

Speaking of which, I've always gotten along much better with females so I couldn't wait to meet and greet Becca. I thought she would surely feel the same and welcome me with open arms. So when Caleb opens the car door, I shoot straight for her, ready to give her a first greeting she will never forget.

Instead of my usual tail wagging, chin-up, tongue-hanging, waiting patiently for the familiar pat on the head, I run full speed at Becca. As she turns to run from me, I pounce, putting my full weight on her fragile back. She immediately stumbles, causing my un-pedicured claws to scratch her from her shoulders down her back to her hips.

She screams. I bark. Through her angry cries, with eyes glaring at Caleb, she mutters, "This isn't going to work." That's when I realize that not all females are the same. Becca may be one of those unusual creatures immune to my canine charms.

ON THE COUCH (Caleb):

I'm not sure why I took this little guy. It must be something on a subconscious level. Maybe he's a lost cause. Maybe he reminds me of when I was in the second grade and wrote on my friend's forehead with an ink pen. As punishment, I was whipped by the principal and sent to stand in the corner. Or maybe, he reminds me of the time my teacher screamed at me for doing the wrong assignment. She turned bright red. I turned bright red. The class shuttered in horror. All the while, my friend laughed hysterically because he had suggested I complete this assignment early, to get extra-credit. Just like Nagi, I was punished for my innocent behaviors.

Or maybe it was because this abandoned dog reminded me of the little black runt I had attached myself to when I was four. The puppy died in my arms at eight-weeks. To this day, this memory continues to haunt me. Anyway, Becca knew I was bringing a dog home and had seemed excited. She always said she was a huge dog lover. I guess she just isn't sure this is the right dog.

CHAPTER TWO

BACKGROUND

I was born one of nine pups. Because I was the runt of the litter, I was often squashed by my pudgy siblings and ignored by my Mom. Come chow time, it was tough to get anything at all.

As the months went on, my attitude was reflected in my life and I vacillated between acting-out and withdrawing. When two-leggers came to break up my family, one-by-one I saw my siblings leave the home. Once they were all adopted, I was left alone with Mom and hoped I would be allowed to remain there with her, even though there was, admittedly, little room for her.

Because of my puppy behaviors, I was placed in a crate for sometimes up to 12 hours a day. When I was released, naturally, I went crazy, chasing my tail and any other thing that moved. To have some peace in the home, my two-leggers generally took me from cramped crate to a small weed-filled backyard space. There were no trees for shade and the foxtails seemed to jump and attach to my thick fur. This only made the two-leggers more aggravated with me.

I felt like the odds were stacked against me so I soon learned to escape and would mosey down the street to the neighborhood pond, where I chased ducks, smashed the tall grasses and nosed bugs along the path. I always came back home after an hour or so of pure entertainment. I was under the delusion that the two-leggers, who in my mind were worried over my absence, would be thrilled to see me again.

Then one day, I overheard the teen boy tell his Mom that he wished I hadn't come back. I was crushed. I guess he was still upset about my tearing a hole in the sleeve of what I considered to be one of his dirtiest and already-tattered sweatshirts.

That's when I knew just how unwelcome I was in my own home. Because of this, I not only continued but increased my escapes. So, in short, I continued to run off, the neighbors continued to complain, and the cat population dwindled (thanks to me, according to some nasty and unfounded rumors).

My escapades forced the two-leggers to place chain-link fencing around the property. Escaping this fortress required my pushing the envelope, my thinking outside the box. Being the clever boy that I am, it didn't take me long to figure out that if I was very careful and raced toward the fencing, I could actually climb the fence and throw myself over to the other side. Given my high poundage, I was pretty impressed with my newfound abilities. The two-leggers saw it much differently, however, and once I was caught in the act, it appeared to be the final straw.

The two-leggers, who I never called my parents because of their apparent lack of concern or love for me, decided enough was enough and took me for a long drive. I was happy to get out of the neighborhood, quite frankly, rarely having the opportunity to enjoy a car ride.

After about 30 minutes, the car suddenly stopped in some strange area, the female got out and I wagged my tail furiously, believing I was being rewarded with a little stroll in unexplored territories. Instead, she jerked me out of the car, quickly got back in, and sped off. Hard as I tried, I couldn't catch up with that car, so there I was, abandoned, confused, alone, hungry, thirsty and more than a little anxious in unfamiliar surroundings. I couldn't help but wonder how a two-legger, so callously and cruelly discarded, would feel under similar circum-stances.

I roamed a little until it got dark, then I hid myself underneath an oleander bush for warmth. My stomach growled all night in hunger. Early the next morning, I was awakened by two medium-sized dogs sniffing me, and then I heard a woman's voice telling them to come.

When I peeked out from a bushy branch, there they were, happily running behind a jogger out for her morning run before starting her work day. This seemed like a happy little group so I decided to join in the fun. The other dogs yelped and nipped, trying to deter me from my spontaneous and, in their minds, unwelcome plan to join the family.

Thankfully, this nice woman took pity on me and took me home, much to the chagrin of the others. Unfortunately, her kindness and patience didn't last long. Because of the continuous nipping, growling and quarreling, I was locked in the garage overnight. Left to my own devices, I entertained myself by tearing up newspaper piles and boxes of Christmas ornaments, and even treated myself to several mouthfuls of black-oiled sunflower seeds, apparently meant for the wild birds.

I naively believed that things would lighten up around there, given time. However, once again, my time was swiftly up. Obviously succumbing to pressure from her other four-leggers, the woman, quite reluctantly she assured me over and over, dumped me at the pound and there I sat until Caleb rescued me that fateful day.

ON THE COUCH (Caleb):

If Nagi thinks his puppyhood was bad, he lived the life of a prince compared to me. Because I was the youngest of seven siblings, I grew up feeling like a lost child in a sea of family. Not only was I ignored, but I was teased incessantly about being a "baby." My older brothers persistently told me that I was the ugliest boy, so much so that I learned to believe it. You see I was born with unpredictable skin rashes and a large growth on my left ear. To me, it looked like a pumpkin was growing out of my head. I always tried to position myself so that only my right profile was exposed, especially when talking to someone (AKA girls) I was trying to impress. My father was a workaholic, spending eight hours a day working the farm, another eight hours working in a factory, and sleeping as much as he could in the few remaining hours. What I craved was to be understood, to feel significant and to look like my Greek-god brothers.

ON THE COUCH (Becca):

I can relate to and appreciate Nagi's escape artistry. I have that self-survival ability, as well, mostly I guess because I was an only child. My father traveled a lot, was hardly home and my mother lived in fantasyland, often escaping into old romantic classics. Some called me a "prima dona" because I came from a wealthy home, but having lots of money isn't all that it's hyped up to be, believe me. Left to my own devices most of the time, I learned to escape into my own world of Barbies that I could dress-up, style-up and invent pretend lives I secretly coveted, like worldwide name recognition and traveling internationally on the arm of a handsome boyfriend. What I really missed, though, was attention and a real connection with just one other person. I was searching for my own version of "Ken" when Caleb unexpectedly showed up and stole my heart.

CHAPTER THREE

NAMED

At first, it seems a typical, ordinary country home. Complete with hundreds of trees upon which to leave my aromatic markers and many acres for me to enjoy at my whimsy. It's definitely not anything like the cramped space I shared in the hustle-bustle of the city. I'm now a mountain dog, living in a small community of no more than 10,000.

Caleb works as a mental health therapist and Becca sells some sort of concoction as a Life Enrichment representative. She's a health nut and he… well he, as it turns out, is just a nut.

The honeymoon period doesn't last long. I sleep on some sissy sunflower pillow, which smells like rancid motor oil and is as lumpy as a sack of potatoes. Something retrieved from a dumpster somewhere, obviously. I know Becca is punishing me for our first encounter and Caleb never seems to have the courage to stand up to her. Still, I never bark, growl or whine in complaint. After all, it's much better than that pound prison. I also notice that my recurring dream is a thing of the past, something I attribute to my new-found freedom.

I'm only home for a couple of days before I'm whisked away to the vet for an overnight stay, following a "so-called" minor surgical procedure. I'm reassured that this surgery is not only for my own good, but for the good of keeping the puppy population down. However, if I had had any part in the decision-making, I would have opted to sire a few pups to continue my bloodline. After all, it's one of the things I do best.

Following my surgery and, thankfully, very quick recovery period, Caleb begins a ritual of taking me for short walks, all the while mumbling something negative about Becca or his job. It never really makes much sense, so I occupy my time searching out squirrels. Becca takes me for longer, out-of-the-way walks. Sometimes I think she is hoping to lose me somewhere along the way. I guess she hasn't figured out that I'm smart enough to find my way back home.

Caleb and Becca are what you might call eclectic parents. When it comes to pinning them down on their attitudes or beliefs, it's near impossible. I think coming up with weird names must be their trademark. They named a cat they rescued Two-Looks. Apparently, they decided that, because this cat was older, mangy and forgotten, no one could appreciate her inner beauty. According to my parents, and I don't know if this true, there's an old Native American saying that goes something like: "To really know someone, you have to take two looks, one with the eyes and the other with the heart." Hence, the name Two-Looks.

Given their thinking, I'm not surprised that I'm saddled with the name, Nagi (Gnah-gee). Apparently, it's a Lakota Indian word. It loosely translates to "intermediary between the material and spirit world." Now I ask you, what on earth does this have to do with me? That's sideways! My parents explain that they expect me to have special qualities, like a spirit dog; maybe possess unique powers… do they actually think I can become invisible?

I prefer to be called Macho, Rufus, Champ or even Killer Kawaski, but maybe this name Nagi will grow on me, I guess ... somehow. I can only imagine the laughter and howling, hooting and hollering should my pound buddies learn of my new name.

ON THE COUCH (Caleb):

So what? What's the matter with projecting my beliefs onto my dog? I want him to be the smartest, most popular, most amazing dog who ever lived. I think it's just a matter of time before we can communicate at a much deeper level. In fact, I think he's already reading some of my thoughts. Last night I was thinking about him wanting to come inside and when I opened the back door, there he was. What a connection we share. Now, if I can just teach him a language we can both understand.

ON THE COUCH (Nagi):

Life is so unfair. What a double standard. At first, there was some idle talk of six weeks of obedience classes, as though I was the one with the destructive behaviors and bad attitude. Thankfully, school never happened, even though Caleb and Becca certainly could have benefitted from some obedience training themselves. On a separate note, I obviously am going to have to amplify my canine behaviors to remind Caleb that I'm a dog. *What have I gotten myself into?*

ON THE COUCH (Becca):

Nagi's really not so bad, after all. He's a good buffer actually, especially since Caleb spends so much time with him. I dearly love Caleb, but this gives me some much-needed space from his constantly analyzing my every behavior. Oh, well. Such is the life of a therapist's wife. As for Nagi's neutering, any responsible parent would do the same.

CHAPTER FOUR

HOME

Becca works part-time selling that health concoction she believes can extend a happy, healthy life. I'm not sure how happy her life is, though, because it seems that she regularly escapes in Marilyn movies. It doesn't appear to be a coincidence that one of her favorites is "Seven Year Itch" and that Becca and Caleb have been married exactly seven years.

Like I mentioned before, Becca is a health nut and thinks everyone should follow her lead. She loves her job, peddling her bottles of magic elixir and hosting silly sales parties where women talk about everything except what they have actually gathered for.

Caleb thinks she can do much better, that she isn't living up to her potential, which is a point of constant contention between them. He often makes fun of her, "Why don't you get a real job?" he asks.

Becca defends herself with, "I love what I'm doing. I'm helping others become healthier, something you wouldn't know anything about."

Now remember, Caleb works in mental health so he considers this a personal attack.

It's obvious my parents fight about the most absurd things. Caleb likes it hot; Becca likes it cold. Caleb wants joint checking accounts; Becca wants to keep the accounts separate. Caleb is a meat-eater; Becca is a die-hard vegetarian. They sleep in separate bedrooms because Becca says Caleb's snoring keeps her awake. Caleb argues that Becca moves around so much, he can't even fall asleep. So, how can he be guilty of snoring?

Such a vicious circle. I soon learn the tell-tale signs of when it's in my best interest to keep my distance. The room will become frosty; Caleb will frown and glare. Becca bites her lower lip to keep from saying something she would later regret. I honestly don't know how these two ever survived seven years of this torture.

ON THE COUCH (Caleb):

Yes, we have our problems. Everyone does, right? I thought once we had Nagi to love, things would change. That didn't happen. Instead, the arguing has escalated. On a positive note, I've noticed that when Becca is upset with me, Nagi lowers his head and glares at her, mimicking my reactions. This tells me he not only understands my side, but agrees with everything I'm saying. Our connection grows stronger. I believe I'm actually experiencing a true male bonding with him.

ON THE COUCH (Becca):

All this arguing is such a waste of time. We have a solid relationship, built on love and trust. This constant bickering doesn't bother me in the least. Besides, I have more important and relevant things on my mind. I have no explanation, but I have developed an overwhelming urge to think, breathe and act Marilyn. Even as a young teen, I had a fascination her. Her vulnerability and innate desire to be liked has always reminded me of myself. In high school, I had her soft, raspy voice down pat, so much so that when I was called upon in class, I responded Marilyn-style… that is, until I grew tired of the negative attention and remarks. As crazy as it sounds, I think I'm actually the reincarnation of Marilyn.

CHAPTER FIVE

GLOP

I freely admit that I'm a meat lover, a carnivore. I crave flesh and bones. This is not difficult to understand. Becca seems to have other ideas. Remember that extreme vegetarian thing? Well, because she's committed to a healthy way of life, she's determined to convert me by introducing "glop" into my diet.

You heard me… "glop." Doesn't that sound appetizing? I think she throws anything she can think of (except meat, of course) in the blender…Wheat Grass, Vitamin B powder, Vitamin C, a dash of Glucasomine, a sprinkle of mysterious Chinese herbs and a dab of plain organic yogurt. She tosses chunky spoonfuls on my dry food and there it sits. That "glop." It doesn't budge. It just sits there, a big unappetizing green dripping mess. (Apparently, the Wheat Grass is to blame for the coloring).

I sit in front of my bowl, looking down at the glop and then up at her, clearly pleading for meat. All to no avail. Being a bit misguided, I innocently believe that if I stare at it long enough, it will magically transform into something I will gladly devour.

But that never happens. What happens is, Caleb takes pity on me, buying chicken. He bastes it with all kinds of seasonings and roasts it in the oven until it smells lick-chopping tasty. Unfortunately, he becomes so overwhelmed by the tempting smells that I have to beg for the scraps. I watch Caleb become territorial as he greedily devours the meat, something logically meant for me. In the meantime, my "glop" becomes greener and heavier in Becca's attempt to lure me into a healthier lifestyle.

Since starvation is definitely out of the question, I do the next best thing in my effort to outsmart her. I teach myself a new trick… I flip my bowl and eat only the dry, untainted food at the bottom. Sadly, that only works for a while. Becca alters her recipe, making the glop runnier and runnier, until every dry morsel has a slimy, green glow.

What's a starving carnivore to do?

ON THE COUCH (Caleb):

Carnivores rule! I remember when Becca tried to get me to eat that "glop." She even tried to disguise it by putting it on her body as part of some sort of romantic ritual. Eventually, she gave up on my conversion, and now focuses her obsession on Nagi. Out of empathy for him, and to appease Becca, I've promised to taste-test each batch, not only to make sure it's edible, but as a brainwashing tool to entice Nagi to eat before he withers away to nothing. Even though I feel sorry for my son (yes, I proudly call him my son now), I'm just not ready to give up my chicken. I have also come to the realization that he needs my protection 24 hours a day. I'll need to bring him to work with me from now on to protect him from this health extremist.

ON THE COUCH (Becca):

I can honestly say that I'm happy with Caleb's selfishness. Nagi doesn't need to eat chicken. The sooner he realizes this fact, the less starved and depressed he will be.

CHAPTER SIX

CO-THERAPIST

Since my rescue, most of my day is spent entertaining myself. I create games like making faces out of clouds, counting how many times I can breathe rapidly without passing out, or racing back and forth along the cattle fence with Sugar Bear, the neighbor dog, who is fat, out-of-shape and a real meathead.

My favorite activity, though, is what I like to call "border patrol." This is where I inspect the property borders in search of uninvited intruders or wanna-be-escapees (squirrels!!!).

There's one squirrel in particular who has caught my attention. He seems to have initiated some game where he shrieks incessantly to announce his presence, then scurries over the rooftop in an effort to goad me into a hot, yet fruitless, pursuit. Even though I never win the game, I continue playing for the sheer thrill of the chase.

Life is good and I thoroughly enjoy my daily routines until Caleb abruptly puts a stop to them, all without asking me if I have other plans.

Caleb used to work in private practice but decided that he wanted an 8 to 5'er with benefits. He says he likes helping people but that he works in a system where managed care, insurances, politics and money dictate his therapy. Long-term therapy is a thing of the past, according to him. Brief therapy is the thing now ... patch'um up and send'um out.

He believes people become therapists to deal with their own issues, insisting that every dedicated therapist should admit to having as many life and relationship problems as their clients. If Caleb's any indication, I'd say he's spot on.

Despite the county's rigid policies about getting paperwork done on time and following the hierarchy of power, the higher-ups surprisingly (and unfortunately for me) have no problem with pets at work. That's how my days switch from lazy delight to head-thumping frustration. I hold hope that my first visit will be my last, that Caleb only wants to show me off, you know like a proud parent showing off his son, but no such luck.

Daily I'm dragged to his office, sitting through endless chattering and hysterical outbreaks about things I have no interest in. In an effort to include me, Caleb often debriefs or consults with me after each session. I'm not surprised considering his therapy style. Typically, I lay next to his swivel chair while Caleb absent-mindedly dangles his hand to tap or pat my head.

As I lazily gaze around the office in boredom, I spot two certificates on the wall, one with Caleb's name as Licensed Marriage Family Therapist and one with my name as co-therapist. What's a co-therapist and how did I become one?

There's also a photo on his desk with some platinum "cotton-candy" blonde. I don't know who it is, but I know it's not Becca. For some peculiar reason, a long yellow pencil is perched against Caleb's coffee cup. Somehow, this setting seems very familiar and disturbing to me, but I'm not sure why.

Day after day, I see different faces but hear the same rhetoric. I come to realize that Caleb, renowned therapist in his own mind, responds the same to everyone. That's sideways! I've always been under the assumption that being a therapist is tough work, but Caleb's style is a no-brainer, which is why I'm a perfect candidate for co-therapist, according to Caleb's chiding. I notice that he seems to ask the same questions during an assessment. What's the presenting problem? Treatment history? Psychosocial history? Medical history? Trauma history? Mental status? Any alcohol or drug history? *B-o-r-i-n-g*!

His empathic responding therapy is a real snoozer. "How are you feeling today? It sounds like… What I hear you saying is…" How many times and different ways does he have to ask someone how they feel? Worse yet, he asks what their triggers or coping skills are. I silently interrupt him with: "Maybe you're the trigger. God knows you certainly trigger me. By the way, if they had coping skills, they wouldn't be sitting here with you, would they?"

It's odd that, no matter what Caleb says or does, these clients keep coming back for more. I like to think I'm the "more," especially since Caleb regularly asks me for input: "Do you think I'm getting through to him? Do you think she trusts me enough to express her feelings about the trauma?"

When he asks a question, I usually react with body movements, which he then interprets to fit his needs at the time. If I lower my head, Caleb interprets that as a "no." If I raise my head, he takes that as a "yes." If I wag my tail, he thinks it's time to move to the next level of treatment. If I yawn, he thinks he's not clear and needs to go over it again with his client. Actually I'm just *b-o-r-e-d*, Caleb. Isn't it time to go home yet?

Gradually, Caleb depends on me during every session for honest feedback. To be perfectly frank, I prefer being home with Becca, even though it means my days will be filled dodging her new and improved veggie glop experiments.

Due to my routine change, along with added counseling responsibilities, it's not surprising that I develop a nervous tic… my left eye twitching uncontrollably. I'm sure that Caleb will eventually take this to mean something it doesn't, as usual. Thanks to Caleb and Becca, I'm well on my way to becoming a neurotic mess.

ON THE COUCH (Caleb):

Maybe I rely too much on Nagi for support, but I know he understands me. We're becoming more and more simpatico, in communication sync. I've been waiting my entire life for someone to come along who completely "gets" me. Who would have thought I would find him at the pound? And about that so-called tic, I call it a wink. It's like we're sharing a secret that's just between us.

ON THE COUCH (Nagi):

Caleb seems to be under the delusion that I'm human. Frankly, I miss being just a dog.

CHAPTER SEVEN

BALLS!

Part of feeling "normal" is balls. What dog doesn't love chasing and fetching balls? More than a hundred thousand years ago, my ancestors, the dinosaurs, retrieved rocks for their masters. Dinosaurs have now been replaced with dogs and rocks replaced with balls.

Caleb loves to watch me fetch. It's not so much the fetching that amuses him, but my trick after fetching. By the way, I don't mean to criticize Caleb (or to demean the entire female gender) but he throws like a girl. No control whatsoever. He keeps tossing them where I have no chance and absolutely no interest in retrieving them. How would you like to dig for a ball in a thorny rose bush?

So this is how the game goes. After I'm exhausted from attempting to fetch and Caleb has developed a sore arm from his pitiful throwing attempts, he leaves me to my own amusement with the last ball.

That's when the real fun begins. I pretend that the ball has a life of its own. I expect it to jump up and bite me or try to run. I drop it from my mouth, and at the same time, place my paw about six inches over it. I then hover and move my paw back and forth teasing it, all the while making low growling sounds, much like a sleepy lion.

My goal is to slap the ball into my salivating mouth. Caleb finds my antics amusing, particularly when I become so animated that I smack the ball too hard with my overzealous touch. So hard that I must pounce before its great escape.

One day I go too far with my ball obsession and have my second, and hopefully last, near-death experience.

What happened, you ask? Well, I'm in the final stages of getting the upper paw in the battle to finally defeat my round opponent, when suddenly, in my enthusiasm, I clamp down on its head and roughly shake it. The next thing I know I have what feels like a pumpkin stuck in my throat.

While I choke on the ball, Caleb and Becca run in circles crying out,

"He's choking. He's choking."

That's a given, isn't it? Why don't they do something to help me? I run in circles, too, more in a panic than for anything else.

Caleb finally scoops me up like a spastic giant and shakes me, trying to dislodge the pumpkin. This only makes matters worse, especially since Becca is in near hysterics and screaming to get me to the car. The vet has been alerted.

Caleb ignores her and gives me the Heimlich maneuver instead. Placing his arms tightly around my chest, he squeezes so hard that I think he's either going to crack my ribs or cause me to have the biggest bowel movement either one of us has ever seen. I'm pretty sure I faint about then. When I come to, the deadly ball rests lifeless in Caleb's hand. I think Caleb is crying.

This is the second time he has saved me from impending death.

ON THE COUCH (Nagi):

What a hero my Dad is. As for me, I know I'm neurotic, but you have to admire my creative genius. When I think about what I see the two-leggers do for entertainment, it's just plain silly… like sitting for hours at a time watching a 55-inch black rectangle with insides that seem to move and talk. Besides, I don't think the ball trick is as neurotic as some of the other things I admit to doing.

CHAPTER EIGHT

PETNAMES

Just as I'm grudgingly adjusting to my work schedule, the family structure crumbles. The arguing becomes relentless. It isn't just the superficial arguments anymore. I overhear them one night, disagreeing about finances. Becca screams, "If you don't like the way I spend my money, find someone else who squanders it like you… better yet, just leave!"

Becca has forgotten that Caleb's father left him when he was only twelve. This is an obvious threat to his security, which shakes him to his very core. It shakes me to my core, too. After all, even though it's pretty dysfunctional, this is my home. (I notice that my head jerks in involuntary violent spasms to the left as I gnaw on my front paw. I apparently have acquired a new way of coping with stress… self-biting.) Caleb fires back, yelling in a voice that sounds more like a wounded ostrich, slams the door, and is nowhere to be found for two days.

Besides going through the trauma of my parent's relationship meltdown, I'm also becoming annoyed and agitated with Caleb's so-called affectionate pet names.

Instead of my proper name of Nagi, he often refers to me as Mr. Pipps, Buddy Boy, Chopper Bopper, Big Man, Blue Balu, Wooley Woo and others I'm too embarrassed to even mention. Because I admire his creativity and it makes me feel important, it seems okay at first. I mentally pretend that he's simply practicing a rap song for Snoopy Dog.

Soon, however, these bizarre pet names grate on my nerves, similar to claws on a chalkboard. The only way I can wrap my head around this nonsense is to mentally counter with my own pet names, so when he calls me Chopper Bopper, I mentally retaliate with Mr. Twit, Killer Bugsby, Fat Man or Toad Head.

Most likely, Caleb thinks the smile on my face is a sign of appreciation for his cleverness, but the truth is that I have created an inner sanctuary where Caleb will never reach me. So much for Caleb's theory that we have a language unto ourselves. He doesn't understand me at all.

ON THE COUCH (Caleb):

Of course I have my silly affectionate pet names. My Mom used to call me Chubby Cubby, Little Brave Man, Cutie Cucumber, and Baby Beetle. I never knew my given name was Caleb until I was ten.

As for the marital turmoil and threats, sure I'm

upset. Nobody likes to be threatened. Maybe I overreact, I don't know. I notice my son becomes frightened when Becca and I fight, but that just shows how emotionally bonded he is with me. I wonder if Becca notices that I'm becoming more attached to Nagi? As for Becca, she's undeserving of pet names.

ON THE COUCH (Becca):

As though I care, Caleb. I've got my own pet name… Marilyn.

CHAPTER NINE

MARILYN

Becca has lost interest in everything other than her obsession with Marilyn. She insists that Caleb refer to her by that name only and I notice that she wastes most of her time studying Marilyn movies and practicing certain catch phrases in front of the bathroom mirror. Almost like she's in a trance.

Caleb has had enough and either ignores her or tells her to "knock it off before he has her hauled off to the 'loony bin.'" Not that I'm any expert, but I think Becca pulls off a pretty good imitation. My thinking is that Caleb is a bit jealous of the attention Becca is taking away from him. After all, her craziness seems to be taking precedence, and Caleb does love the limelight.

One day, Becca decides to go to the extreme, bleaching her brunette hair platinum blonde and re-styling it to resemble a big white ball of cotton candy. She adds bright red lipstick and a low-cut skintight sweater to complete her look. Caleb practically drools when she walks in, which only serves to feed her delusion. By the way, I always thought drooling was reserved for dogs and babies.

This goes on for a short while until Caleb is forced to snap "out of it" when Becca dons a diamond ring with matching multi-caret diamond necklace. Becca has now hit him where it hurts the most… his wallet. He confronts her, expressing his concern that she's having a psychotic break and his worry that she's taking this Marilyn "hobby" a bit too far.

Becca patiently waits until Caleb has finished and then calmly announces that she has no control in the matter. She is reluctantly possessed by the spirit of Marilyn. This is much more than a "hobby."

She goes on to explain that Marilyn has been waiting for a new body and that she was chosen because hers is so pure. Devoid of all toxins, thanks to the Life Enrichment formula. She further insists that should I continue with my veggie glop diet, Lassie may find me the perfect receptacle.

Immediately embarrassed and remorseful she has let the cat-out-of-the-bag, Becca pleads for Caleb's silence on her alter personality. To placate Caleb (and to bribe him into silence), Becca agrees to return the diamond ring. She will not, however, return the necklace since she says it was purchased on clearance and is non-returnable. She adds that she will not be seeking any therapeutic treatment, because after seeing Caleb's "so-called self-improvement," she no longer believes in it.

ON THE COUCH (Becca):

I'm sure my obsession with Marilyn may seem a bit odd to you, but who turns a normal dog into a co-dependent, neurotic co-therapist?!? I ask you ... who's crazier? In my opinion, it's Caleb and now he's trying to drag Nagi down with him. I've got to come up with a plan not only to save Nagi, but to get Caleb to spend more alone time with me, to save this marriage.

As for this Marilyn thing, maybe I have a touch of Delusional Disorder, but I assure you, I'm not crazy. Marilyn speaks to me and through me every day. I guess some people are simply chosen to carry out certain missions, kind of like a life purpose. My mission is obviously Marilyn. She was not finished here ... this, I know is true. She just told me so yesterday.

ON THE COUCH (Nagi):

Who's Lassie?

CHAPTER TEN

MOBSTER

It's one of those rare days when Caleb is on time and we may actually get out of the office by five ... that is, until someone unexpected arrives to throw off our schedule.

A stocky man, medium-sized with wild eyes, a thick unkempt beard and heavy accent, bursts in to Caleb's office. Startled, Caleb confronts him, advising him that he will need to make an appointment just like everyone else. Instead of leaving, the man plops on the couch, sizing Caleb up without uttering a word.

Caleb again insists that he leave immediately. The man jumps up and with no warning, roughly pushes Caleb against the desk. "You may not know who I am, but I definitely know who you are."

Caleb responds defiantly, "Well, as flattering as that may be, I'm booked solid this afternoon. No openings until next week."

The man then shoves Caleb into the nearby chair. "We'll get along much better if you cut out the wise cracks. I'm Gilbertoh, the older brother of Maria Cabre-rro. I'm sure you recognize that name. I made a lengthy trip from Mexico City just to see you and here you are, wanting me to leave without giving me the courtesy of hearing me out, not very hospitable of you now, is it?"

It's obvious to me that Caleb not only recognizes the name, but fear seems to ooze from every pore of his body. I'm not sure Gilbertoh is aware enough to notice the slight change in Caleb's stance, though. He actually seems more pre-occupied in watching himself in the mirror, as he struts around the office, knocking orna-mental items and reference books off the shelves.

"Let's cut to the chase, shall we? Maria told me all about you. You're the only one who really cared or listened to her. She said that, with you, she was finally able to be herself. That she didn't feel judged, no matter what. And what did you do with that trust? You took advantage of her, using your influence to have her committed. Not quite the Prince Charming she made you out to be, are you now?"

This Gilbertoh doesn't seem too smart. Of course, Caleb is no Prince Charming. That would only be possi-ble if he ate veggie glop, right? Caleb remains stone-like. Sitting in silence, trying to maintain his poker face. It's almost painful to watch.

"While I love Maria, I honestly know she can be a little crazy, so I'm okay with her being locked up for a while. What I'm not okay with is the matter of a missing locket. Know anything about that?"

"Locket?" Caleb is becoming more alarmed as Gilbertoh anxiously paces the office. Apparently, this Maria was before my time. In my naiveté, I think I know what's going on here. Caleb has told me all about transference, where a client thinks she's in love with her therapist. This must be an extreme case.

"Si, locket. A little something Maria never removed, not even when she showered. Yet, we are here today because she is no longer in possession of that locket. I will stop at nothing to get it back. *Nada. Nothing.* If you value your life and that of your little sidekick over there, I'd return that locket pronto. Do I make myself crystal clear?"

"Honestly, Mr. Gilbertoh, I don't know what you're talking about," Caleb pleads. "Yes, I remember Maria, but we were never involved in a relationship other than purely professional. As for a locket, I don't even remember her wearing one to our sessions."

"Now, that's very interesting. Maria mentioned in one of her letters how you had taken a shine to it. Like I said, I want that locket returned, and I believe you are just the person who can accomplish that special delivery. You were the last person to have any kind of personal relationship with my sister and from the sounds of her letters, she confided in you as to why that locket is so important to me and my boys."

"Really…" Caleb is roughly cut off when Gilbertoh places his index finger to his mouth. "You really only have two choices. Either get me that locket or come up with $100,000 as compensation. If you are not able to do either, well, I guess you do have a third choice," Gilbertoh chuckles … "to suffer torture and a *muy* slow death. *Comprende*?"

With that, Gilbertoh waves a gun that is so small, it looks more like a toy under Caleb's large nose. Caleb, doesn't seem to notice the size.

"Out of respect for Maria, I'll give you three months to make things right. Don't worry about contacting me, I'll find you." Gilbertoh turns on his heels, gives me a quick pat on the head, and races out the door. It seems like several minutes before Caleb takes a deep breath, more like releasing a relieved sigh.

"Nagi, what am I going to do?" Caleb admits that he did have the locket in his possession, he had taken it from Maria to keep it safe during her hospitalization. He was on his way to the bank to put it into the safety deposit box when he was mugged. His wallet, watch and briefcase were stolen. Inside the briefcase was the locket. He didn't admit this to Gilbertoh because he knew the truth sounded more like a lie. Besides, according to Caleb, Maria warned him about Gilbertoh, a *muy malo*, drug-affiliated thug.

ON THE COUCH (Gilbertoh):

I can't believe I actually pulled it off. From the look on the shrink's face, I'd say he's pretty scared of me right now. I was watching myself in the mirror, and I must admit that I even scared myself a little. I didn't even recognize myself. I only hope Caleb is afraid enough to follow through with returning that locket. I honestly don't know what I'll do if he doesn't come through. I don't think Caleb is aware of what treasures that key unlocks, but it means everything to me.

My great-grandmother's recipe for spicy, fire-roasted salsa is the key to my future. It can open the door for me as I pursue my dream of attending culinary school in Spain, and starting my own authentic Mexican restaurant. Think of it ... Chef Gilbertoh. A nice ring, don't you think?

My family and thug friends still believe I'm wrapped up in this drug thing, but the truth is, I found my real passion in prison… cooking. It was thrilling creating delicious dishes that my fellow inmates raved about. I never got that kind of respect on the streets, and I've always had a deep-seated urge to prove myself. Now that opportunity is so close ... I can almost taste it.

Speaking of family, I've got to remember to get this gun back to my nephew's toy box. It's crazy just how real toy guns look these days.

ON THE COUCH (Caleb):

You're probably wondering why I never filed a police report when I was mugged. I can answer in one word: fear. Even Maria talked about her family with fear in her voice. She warned me many times about their intimate connection with the Mexican drug lords. She also confided that Gilbertoh, upon his release from prison, would definitely come looking for the locket, which holds the key to a bus terminal locker.

Even though Maria doesn't seem to know what the locker actually contains, my guess is that it's illegal drugs or wads of hundreds, given Gilbertoh's criminal background. And him tossing his weight around and threatening me only confirms my suspicions.

Even though he's pretty menacing, definitely means business, I have something he doesn't ... Nagi as protection.

ON THE COUCH (Nagi):

Huh?

CHAPTER ELEVEN

YOSEMITE

As Becca and Caleb grow further and further apart, I quite literally become man AND woman's best friend and somehow, become the sounding board in their relationship.

Becca spends the better part of her evening complaining about Caleb. Every evening. And not only does Caleb take me into his confidence regularly about his marital woes, he plans his vacations to include me ... without Becca.

Our first outing is a four-day camping trip. Becca doesn't seem to mind that she isn't invited. She probably thinks it's a guy thing, you know, a male bonding ritual.

Caleb decides to go to the higher elevations of Yosemite, above Tuolumne Meadows. We pack the usual camping gear, a cook stove, lanterns, sleeping bags, pup tent ... let me stop right here. What a demeaning insult to our youth, associating a tent with a pup. That's sideways!

Little did I know that this trip is a ruse to allow

Caleb enough solitude to plot and calculate the perfect murder. Of course, he needs me as a consultant, so this trip is all about him. God only knows how much I need and deserve some R&R.

Before I forget how it's done, I had wanted to do the typical four-legger activities: chasing squirrels, nosing for ants and other bugs in the dirt, or rolling in the cool water against the rocks until my spots rub off.

Did I mention I have black spots? It's like someone has thrown a can of black paint at me, causing dark splotches to land in no particular order on my white face and ears. Caleb often teases me about this, asking in one of his weaker attempts to impersonate an Englishman: *"Did God paint your face?"* I just look up at him. Apparently, no answer is needed or required.

Anyway, I digress. On this trip, there's no roaming or exploring. Except for the routine potty breaks, my fun consists of sitting by Caleb's side as he talks incessantly about his treacherous and devious plot against Mom. It's like he's not only trying to convince me, but also trying to make sense of it all in his own twisted mind.

When Caleb first tells me he has no choice but to murder Becca, I'm so shocked I cough, which triggers my tic, which triggers my self-biting. Worse yet, Caleb mistakes, as he often does, my violent head jerking as a "yes", that I am offering my total support. Little does he know, or care, that I'm howling inside.

Caleb explains there are two good reasons for murdering Becca, the first, he insists, involves our unexpected office visitor last month. The second, he whispers as he cups my whiskery chin in his hand, gazing into my coal-black eyes, "Sport, I love you. You're the only one who truly gets me."

I cough so badly that I swallow a circling horse fly.

Caleb then proclaims a bonus to this scheme is the term life insurance policy of one million dollars, of which, he is the sole beneficiary. That will take care of Gilbertoh with plenty left over. Besides, he says I should be glad to be rid of Becca, given my near starvation diet of "glop." My Mom, in his opinion, is turning me into a passive, pathetic vegetarian with no ambition.

I'll never understand why I didn't experience a full-blown panic attack, then and there. Instead, my tics and self-biting will have to calm my nerves for the time being.

Around the evening campfire, Caleb explains that the idea for Becca's demise came to him following Gilbertoh's visit. He insists that Gilbertoh could prove to be the perfect patsy, given his criminal background and recent threats.

With that, Caleb jots down free-flowing, random murder scenarios on an ordinary yellow legal size notepad:

1) poisoning Becca's health drink; 2) training me to turn the steering wheel while traveling at high speeds; his thinking is that with Becca driving, I take control of the wheel, aim the car off the road and over a cliff (of course, at the last second, I safely bail out). Has he been watching too many late night movies? That's sideways! 3) while trying to avoid hitting me in the driveway, he accidentally runs over Becca; 4) dig a bunker, hit Becca over the head with a shovel and bury her deep inside. (Caleb has always wanted a bunker for storage and protection in case of a nuclear or terrorist attack so he believes the bunker could possibly serve multiple purposes); 5) and lastly, stage a fake burglary, where Caleb mistakenly shoots Becca, not the imaginary robber.

These last two plots bring a twinkle to Caleb's eye and a sinister laugh bellows from deep within, suggesting he's proud of himself and prizes these two ideas best.

ON THE COUCH (Caleb):

I know what you're thinking. How can an even-tempered, near-brilliant therapist be duped by dangerous thugs? Or maybe you're wondering how I can possibly betray my wife for the love of a dog? Since I believe anyone can be duped if they are in the right place at the wrong time, I won't bother with the first question.

As for the second, all my life, I have wanted to be with someone who really loves me, understands me and accepts me. Isn't that what we all want? Who says that "person" has to be a person? I really can't help it that Nagi is the only one for me. Think about it. Would you rather spend your life being miserable in a dead-end marriage or with man's best friend? Besides, that insurance cash will come in handy now that Gilbertoh is breathing down my neck.

ON THE COUCH (Nagi):

Even though he blames it on Gilbetoh, I was always curious how Caleb came up with the actual idea to murder Becca. It just seems so out of character. My curiosity is answered one night a few months after our camping trip, while sitting as a loving family watching the movie "Niagra" with Marilyn. The plot involves a wife planning her husband's demise. Unbeknownst to the wife, her husband has devious plans of his own. I wonder if Becca has plans for Caleb.

ON THE COUCH (Becca):

Does he really think I don't know what he's up to? Does he really think I haven't noticed how he excludes me every chance he gets? Well, I've come up with a little plan to get Caleb to pay more attention to me, to actually need me again. Little does he know that while he's been busy poisoning Nagi's mind against me, I've been busy doing some poisoning of my own. Caleb has absolutely no idea that I've been slowly adding a special little ingredient for his consumption alone ... small rationings of rat poison carefully concealed in his veggie glop taste test.

Now, don't get me wrong. I'm not trying to kill him, only make him so sick that he has to rely on me to take care of him. Hopefully, this will lead to our re-connecting on a deeper level.

CHAPTER TWELVE

MENTOR

No one can imagine what I'm going through. My head is cloudy and my emotions run rampant. On the one paw, I'm expected to participate in Caleb's murder plot, and on the other, despite her idiosyncrasies, Becca is the only real mother I have ever known.

I find myself in a constant state of turmoil and anguish. I need an outlet to rest from the insanity of my life. I want to scream, "I'm just a dog, you know… a d-o-g," but I know my pleas will fall on deaf ears so I decide to entertain myself by digging through the neighbor's trash instead. She always has great meaty leftovers. I'm salivating just thinking about the treasures awaiting me.

That's when I met Rex… the one who will become my confidante, my mentor, my escape planner. He bears a name I always thought should have been mine… Rex. Such a regal name, don't you think? A name befitting a dog such as myself, but I wouldn't say its namesake was very regal or upper-crust at all.

The chance meeting comes about as the result of my unsatisfied appetite and greediness to find every last delectible morsel, and of course, to infuriate the neighbor woman at the same time… such fun. However, when I flip the last trash can lid with my nose, I fall back startled, becoming twisted in the unappetizing trash I had strewn from previously destroyed trash bags.

"Hey put that lid back on, will ya? I'm trying to perfect my wheelies and you're hampering my style." I peek over the side of the can, and there standing arrogantly on six tiny roller skates, wearing a backwards baseball cap is what looks like a black squishy bug, the kind I play with before meals. I reach in, mouth open wide to make the snatch, when he kicks me square on the tip of my nose. I howl in pain.

"Hey, I barely tapped you and only did so to protect myself. I've learned over the years that it's harder to munch on a creature once you know its name, so, before you get any funny ideas like using me as an appetizer, let me introduce myself," he says while bowing. "I am Rex the Scarabaeidae. That would be Sir Rex Maxwellian to you as I come from a long line of scarab beetles… going all the way back to the days of the pharaohs. My father, Osos, actually sat beside King Tut and acted as his advisor."

I'm not sure who King Tut is, but I'm thinking he could be related to Queen Mutt, my pal from the old neighborhood.

"So, as you see, given my royal lineage, an appetizer I am not."

Sir Rex is now reclining against a chocolate wrapper, all six legs crossed and skates swinging aimlessly in mid-air. "Not only am I most assuredly not a tasty mouthful, but I have much wisdom to share and lessons to teach, so let's think of this little trash heap as the classroom for our first lesson, shall we?"

I tilt my head to one side as if trying to make sense of his ramblings. This only encourages him to continue. In that respect, he reminds me of Caleb.

"Beetles such as myself have the biggest hearts of all creatures, which is why we lug around these thick outer shells. That way, no one can spot our soft underbellies. The shell is there to protect our talking hearts ... so, to my point ... once again, how can something so amazing as myself be even remotely categorized a food item?"

Noticing my confusion, Rex decides to take a more direct approach.

"From the looks of you, you certainly could benefit from my worldly experience and vast wisdom. Just as my great father before me, I humbly offer my services. I'm quite the star and have all the right connections so if it turns out that I can't help you, I can definitely hook you up with someone who can.

"Just to give you a hint of my star power, in my last

movie with Batman, the director wanted me to play Robin, but that cape was just too much to handle. My athletic little legs kept getting tangled up in it. Besides with a face like mine, why hide behind a mask? Batman, yes… but Sir Rex Maxwellian… oh no, no, no. You should see Batman without his hours of make-up… not nearly as handsome as myself.

"Hey, why so quiet… cat got your tongue?" I just sit there, eyes glazed and mouth slack-jawed. Again, Rex takes my silence as a cue to continue.

"Back to that shell thing I mentioned earlier, I can tell that you have a shell, too. If you aren't true to yourself, or if you don't say and show what you feel, you are destined to create and lug around a heavy, burdensome shell. Your feelings kind of get stuck and you get all tangled up inside. Not speaking up, not being true to your innate nature causes all kinds of internal problems.

"Why I actually remember when my shell began growing. It was a few years ago when Nike approached me and NBA star Stephen somebody, about some national advertising gig." I must appear comatose at this point. Rex either doesn't catch the physical cues or simply doesn't care and so the ramblings of the mad beetle persist.

"Stephen was thrilled to be working with me, of course, but I found him to be a bit overbearing and quite jealous of my good looks. Plus, his wife relentlessly flirted with me… obviously smitten with what she saw. Happens everywhere I go, but what's a handsome scarab to do?

"Anyway, I was looking quite dapper that day. Stephen only had two Nikes on his big overgrown feet, whilst I had on six tiny pairs in different, yet complimentary colors. His wife practically passed out with the sight of me. And don't think Stephen didn't notice the chemistry thickly permeating the air. Do you know what he did next?"

Obviously, no response is needed. "He deliberately stepped on two of my little feet, causing them to swell instantly. I tried to retaliate by pinching his big toe, but those Nikes definitely live up to their reputation and were practically impenetrable. Limping to my dressing room, I knew the show must go on, as anyone of my star quality realizes, and I asked for two Nikes in a larger size to hide my now completely misshapen, black-and-blue feet. Nike accommodated by strapping the tennies on tighter than the first time to try and make me look more proportioned. The result was that my two already swollen feet swelled even more, to more than twice my body size. You heard me right… *twice my body size.* Can you imagine?"

"Excuse me, Sir Rex," I interrupt. "I have trash to strew and leftovers to devour. Besides I have to get to bed early tonight because I have a long work day tomorrow."

"Work day?"

"I'm a co-therapist. Anyway, that's what Caleb, my Dad, calls me."

"You poor kid. No time to just be yourself, huh? Just remember what I told you. Even though you appear to be unimpressed with my star quality, it's obvious to me that you are beginning to develop a gigantic shell. You're a four-legger with a heavy heart. Lots of problems. You've forgotten who you are. Once you learn to listen to your heart, with a bit of luck you can stay true to your path and not stray again. Oh, and drop the 'Sir.'"

As I head home, I turn and holler over my shoulder, "You never asked, but I'm Nagi."

ON THE COUCH (Rex):

Nagi didn't have to tell me his name. I already knew. You must be asking yourself how I know so much. Well, it's my line of work and by now you already know about my royal lineage. What I didn't tell you is that Nagi and I have crossed paths before, and as hard as it is to believe, he doesn't seem to remember me. All is well, though. I know our special connection will come back to him, under my patient tutelage. The honest truth, though, is that I can read anyone, no matter if there is a prior relationship and no matter how many legs are attached to their bodies.

My special gifts are intuition and heightened emotional and mental sensitivity. In fact, before Oprah courted Dr. Phil, I was his main confidant and supporter. I can't count on my 18 toes how many times he came to me for advice in his personal struggles and with client issues. Following his fame and good fortune, and not wanting to share the spotlight or glory, he immediately cut me out of the picture.

ON THE COUCH (Nagi):

Rex seems familiar to me somehow. I just can't remember where I've seen him before. I also don't remember him talking so much.

CHAPTER THIRTEEN

DREAMTIME

I can usually make no sense of my dreams, much less remember them in vivid detail. However, these days, I'm not sure if my mind is playing tricks, as my dreams seem to be as real as the craziness in my life. Because of this, I'm having difficulty distinguishing between what's real and what isn't.

My latest involves me lying on the lawn minding my own business when I hear what I believe to be a squirrel scurrying across the roof, which is really no big deal. It happens all the time. However, this particularly pesky squirrel is not your average pest. As he runs back and forth, jumping from poplar branch to rooftop, he comes to a sudden halt and yells out, "Hey Lazy Bones. Up here."

I slowly raise my eyes to see the squirrel dressed like a penguin, complete with top hat, which barely covers his protruding ears. He also has the bushiest tail, biggest belly and curliest whiskers that I have ever seen on similar varmints.

"I'm Sideways and I have an important message for you." I'm honestly mesmerized by the sight of this silly-looking creature. I've finally come to accept Rex, but now this? And how is it that this creature is named after my signature catch-phrase, "That's sideways?"

Suddenly, I spot a red turtle waddling across the roof and onto the long, outstretched poplar limb. Other than its color, size and the huge grin on its face, the turtle looks normal. He reminds me of a zoo turtle, you know the ones who move so slowly that it almost looks as though they're motionless.

Anyway, this clumsy turtle is attempting to walk across a thin, stringy poplar branch. About three steps into it, he falls, crashing to the lawn just a few feet in front of me, belly-up.

"Please help me. Quick, turn me over or I will surely die." Given his enormous size, I hunch up on my back legs and with all my strength, struggle to turn the fat turtle right-side-up. Before I can succeed, I hear the loudest heartbeat I've ever heard. The **thump, thump, thump** is almost deafening. Next I see the whole inside of its heart light up, bursting forth like bright red fireworks in a darkened sky. I peer into the sparkling light and to my shock I see myself as a small puppy, happily pushing and playing with my sisters and brothers. I remember this as one of the few times in my life that I was allowed to be a *dog*.

Sideways, who has been observing this interaction, whispers loudly, "Never forget who you are, my friend." And with that, he and the turtle seem to disappear.

Later that day, more to amuse Rex than anything else, I tell him about my dream.

ON THE COUCH (Rex):

Just how do I get through to Nagi? He's under the delusion that his encounter with Sideways is just a ridiculous dream. In an attempt to enlighten him, I tell him that maybe there is indeed a message from Sideways, something he needs to pay special attention to. I carefully lay it all out for him, explaining that perhaps he had this dream because he is at a crossroads, one where he must be true to himself and listen to his heart, rather than falling deeper into the role-playing of his two-leggers.

ON THE COUCH (Sideways):

Okay, I admit that my entrance may be a little over-dramatic, but I'm up for whatever it takes to "wake" a fellow four-legger. Hopefully, Rex will shake him up a little bit more.

ON THE COUCH (Nagi):

While all squirrels look alike, Sideways resembles one particular squirrel (minus penguin suit) who lounges on our redwood deck most mornings. As he stands and leans full-weight against the horizontal wood beam, much like two-leggers leaning over a balcony, he seems to be enjoying the view. Because the deck is off-limits, he stays just out of my grasp. Now this dream has me wondering if I'm the "view." And if so, why?

CHAPTER FOURTEEN

WORK

Some days I look forward to going to the office; most days I don't. One of my favorite memories is working with Caleb in the counseling of one of his more bizarre cases, Penny (not her real name). Her presenting problem was her fear of leaves falling on her head, which would then cause her scalp to burn as if on fire. Of course, when she first told us this, Caleb and I looked at each other, waiting for the other to bust out laughing. Fortunately, somehow we contained ourselves and remained professional.

After about six unsuccessful sessions with Caleb trying everything he knew (which granted, wasn't much), he looked down at me and right there in front of Penny asked in a desperate voice, "What would you do to help her, Nagi?" By this time, I was standing instead of sitting because we were getting down to some serious business here.

For some unknown reason, probably because of the intense pressure I was under, I spontaneously went into a violent tic, almost breaking my neck. My "ticking" apparently frightened Penny, who screamed because she thought I was heading into bite-mode. When she screamed, my head jerked again and I automatically lifted my leg and peed on her obviously name-brand, very expensive shoes.

The room momentarily became quiet as Caleb and Penny stared at each other dumb-founded. I bowed my head in humiliation. Suddenly the room erupted in laughter. They laughed so hard and so long that I believed they were close to hyperventilating.

Because Penny never returned, Caleb convinced himself that this was actually a therapeutic intervention for her. He almost had me convinced, too, until he received a bill for $1,200 to replace her Pradas, along with a curt note stating she had found a more qualified and more professional therapist. Even worse, for Caleb, there was also a postscript thanking me for all my insight and patience during our last session.

Then came the day I evolved into a true co-therapist. Caleb had a new client, Betty. She came to the office with her hands trembling, acting as though she could bolt at any moment. Caleb, in his mechanical, yet empathetic way, asked her to sit down and relax. There was a lengthy silence before she finally squeaked out: "I've never done this before and am a little uncomfortable talking to someone I don't know."

Caleb, without first consulting me, naturally, said,

"This is my therapy dog, Nagi. Would you like to talk to him instead, to be alone with him until you feel more comfortable?" She nodded and Caleb left the office, saying that he would check back in about 15 minutes.

Well, here I am alone with a perfect stranger. Because I didn't know whether she would pet me or kick me, I held my ground... waiting for her first move. She sat anxiously on the couch and immediately began rubbing my ears while humming a tune I didn't recognize.

After about five minutes, my ears felt ironed to my head and I was beginning to develop another nervous tic, which caused her to stop. She then proceeded to pat me on the head. This pat was more like someone trying to crack the shell of a walnut, which caused me to bite my right leg until it began to bleed. Seeing my discomfort, along with tiny specks of blood dotting the carpet, she backed off from physical contact completely and bemoaned her life.

Her story was indeed a tale of woe. Her husband had just left her. She had lost her home to foreclosure and had just undergone major surgery for a brain tumor. The next thing I knew, it was raining. I didn't understand how that was possible, until I realized it was Betty crying... not crying really, more like wailing.

This made me feel very uncomfortable. However, if there is one thing I have learned from Caleb, it's counter-transference. I couldn't let my feelings affect my client. I had to be supportive during her flood of emotions. In fact, I believed I was the catalyst for some serious, intrapsychic, traumatic reprocessing of pain and suffering.

Suddenly, and at the worst possible moment, Caleb flung open the door. He must have been outside listening the entire time. In a jealous rage and thinking I had somehow upstaged the master, Caleb grabbed Betty's hand and patted her back. "Are you OK, Betty? Can I sit with you now?" She nodded. Caleb locked me in the next room, and took over the rest of the session.

ON THE COUCH (Nagi):

So much for co-therapy.

ON THE COUCH (Caleb):

I can't believe this little traitor, this upstart wanabe therapist. Doesn't he realize that Betty was ready to explode, that anyone could have easily produced the same therapeutic benefits? I'm the real therapist here and if he knows what's good for him, he'll keep his place and never, *ever* try to outshine my skill or wisdom.

On the other hand, if I can somehow put my jealousy aside for the moment, I can honestly say I'm rather proud of him. Nagi could have bitten Betty or even scratched the door demanding that I release him. He is becoming more like me every day. He does what he needs to do to get the job done.

I'm actually grateful I had him take over for me today, especially since my stomach has been bothering me a great deal lately. It must be the stress I'm under; the apprehension of knowing what's coming for Becca…

Soon, my love, soon.

CHAPTER FIFTEEN

SCHEME

By now, Caleb is fully committed to Becca's murder. He has come to the conclusion that it will not only solve any financial problems, but will also take care of that ominous thug, Gilbertoh. The time of the nefarious act is set. Becca will die in two months.

The plan is simple. At least in theory. Caleb will rent a movie and prepare a vegetarian delight for Becca. He really only knows how to make one dish, pasta with steamed vegetables. He will be totally attentive, romantic and appreciative of her. After all, it was to be her last meal. That's sideways!

During dinner, Caleb will encourage Becca to drink at least three glasses of wine. Once she is completely relaxed, he will knock over lamps and chairs while retrieving the revolver secretly stashed in the lawn-mower grass catcher. That's my cue to bark.

Because of all the commotion, Caleb anticipates that Becca will jump out of bed dazed and in a fog, stumble down the hall, calling Caleb's name. From the garage door, Caleb will yell out, "There's a burglar in the house. Get out."

When he hears Becca running down the hallway, he will be able to pinpoint her position in the darkness, and then "accidentally" shoot her, mistaking her for the non-existent intruder.

The paramedics will be called, but will tragically arrive too late. Becca will be pronounced dead at the scene. Caleb will perform his part and casually mention Gilbertoh's name as a possible suspect, a criminal bent on revenge for his sister and obsessed with not only destroying Caleb's career, but ruining his life. He will, of course, act the grieving spouse for an appropriate period before collecting the insurance money.

Caleb believes his plot is foolproof, that Gilbertoh's office visit is truly good fortune. Even though, I want more than anything to follow my heart and save Becca, I believe I have no choice but to go along with Caleb's plan. After all, he has reminded me countless times that if I don't cooperate, I will no longer be his co-therapist or, more importantly, his son.

You can't picture how badly I feel, to be part of a murder plot against someone I love. The details of her last day, a grand meal before her unjustified execution, reminds me of my final day at the pound, and I can't help but empathize with her and hope someone comes to her rescue, just like Caleb came to mine. Secretly, I anticipate that Caleb will chicken out or miss the shot, or that Becca will suffer only a surface wound, discover Caleb's plot and retaliate in kind.

ON THE COUCH (Rex):

Nagi, I'm listening and can appreciate your pain and suffering. I know you're really torn between your parents. Why I remember when my Uncle Max was torn at Waterloo. He had to make a decision, either to fight beside his buddy, General Francoise (definitely a losing battle), or race to find a large rock to hide under for protection, to wait out Francoise's demise. I forgot to tell you that Uncle Max's role was General of Strategic Very Low Ground Tactics or GSLGT, as it is more commonly called. Well, Uncle Max loved both Napoleon and Francoise, but he had to choose… and fast. He chose survival and ran like the wind, saving himself.

(*Nagi*): "So, you're saying I'm supposed to run? Abandon Becca when she needs me the most?" I scratch my head in bewilderment. Rex jumps back, clearly thinking I am flea-infested.

(*Rex*): "All I can do is offer the wisdom, Nagi. How you interpret it is up to you." *Don't tell Nagi, but even I'm not sure what my point is ... sometimes, I just love to hear the sound of my own voice.*

ON THE COUCH (Caleb):

I don't know what's going on with me. I'm not sleeping and I have nonstop stomach pains. Becca has discouraged me from seeking medical attention, insisting that I've been working too hard lately and that all I need is some good old-fashioned R&R and some extra TLC from her. Maybe she's right.

ON THE COUCH (Becca):

I may have to decrease the poison dosage a bit, maybe take it a little slower. It will definitely spoil my plans if Caleb sees the doctor.

CHAPTER SIXTEEN

GRR-R-R-R

Life goes on as usual and my Mom's impending doom is not discussed. By now, I have resentfully accepted my fate as Caleb's co-therapist. What I will never get used to, however, is growl therapy.

I guess Caleb got the idea from some primal scream therapy book. Besides he is a product of the 60s, which makes him a little deranged from all the drugs he has ingested. Honestly, I'm not sure how therapeutic it is or who it's supposed to "cure" since the only participants are Caleb and I.

Anyway, Caleb sits on the couch and growls. I usually have two options at this point: to immediately run from this lunatic, who is obviously inept at imitating me, or just go along with it and see where it goes. By choosing the second option, I have the chance to get the upper paw and even nip at Caleb, which wouldn't be my fault, since he started the whole growl therapy thing.

The routine goes something like this. Caleb gets my attention, bares his teeth, wrinkles his nose and with his brow crinkled in a deep frown, growls in a low tone. I have no alternative but to reciprocate and growl back in an even lower tone with a deeper furrowed brow.

Caleb becomes louder. I become louder. This escalates into a barking frenzy, no holds barred. At some point, we both have saliva dripping from our mouths and glazed-over eyes.

Finally, when I am out of control and just about to lose it completely, Caleb stops, folds his hands in his lap, and sits there triumphantly with a silly grin on his face, knowing he has got me… again. Like a fool, I fall for it every time… so damn humiliating, especially since my IQ has to be higher than his.

ON THE COUCH (Caleb):

You know how much I love Nagi. These tests build character, as well as reminding him who's boss. I know he will never actually bite me and it's good therapy for me to get my anger out. I would much rather take it out on Becca, but I don't want her to leave me before I have my chance to murder her. Besides, I know **she** bites.

ON THE COUCH (Rex):

That's some twisted father you have, Nagi. I can't believe he would intentionally set you up like that. It reminds me of the time I was deliberately set up while shooting a movie with Robert and Julia in England. I was Robert's double as a stunt driver.

Well, let me get quickly to my point. He convinced me that Julia was hot for my body and that after the last scene was shot, she wanted to meet me in the Jacuzzi. So like a fool, I waited in the spa, in my birthday suit, au natural, surrounded by lit candles, wine and Zimbabwe tribal music.

After waiting for about an hour, becoming drunk as a skunk, and singing rhythmic tribal music at the top of my lungs, in walked Robert with the entire cast, laughing their heads off.

Unbeknownst to me, Robert had been filming and was planning to dub my spa behaviors, which were admittedly a bit embarrassing, into the last scene of the movie. Fortunately, it never happened because of my threat of a lawsuit.

Julia felt so guilty about her part, she promised to name her first male child after me. Per my attorney's instructions, I can't discuss this any further due to the impending lawsuit for Julia not living up to her promise. So my point is, dear Nagi, think lawsuit.

CHAPTER SEVENTEEN

ALOHA

By now, I'm sure Becca knows that Caleb loves me and prefers my company. To rub salt in the relationship wound, he takes me to romantic Hawaii for 10 days, where we stay in a thatched cottage overlooking the sea.

Since Caleb has been pushing me hard as his co-therapist and devoted best friend, my idea of a perfect vacation is geared towards relaxation. I plan on finding a comfy hammock, hanging between two isolated coconut trees, and hooking up with other four-leggers, who are rumored to be true island party animals.

Once again, however, Caleb has other ideas. He signs us up, without asking of course, for surfing lessons, hula dancing, Hawaiian cooking class, a jungle trek to a well-known pineapple plantation, a helicopter tour of the islands and snorkeling. Now, this is all within the first couple of days, mind you. I'm exhausted just thinking about it.

I'll spare you all the details of this unbearable trip to "paradise" and give you instead an overall glimpse.

Surfing does not go well. I'm sure you have seen other magnificent dogs riding surfboards. Admittedly, these stars are pretty amazing and I'm actually a bit envious of their coordination, but, in my defense, I've never been to the ocean, much less ridden a "board."

So after countless wipe-outs, I finally perch perfectly on my board as my drill sergeant orders. In his typical fashion, Caleb isn't a bit sensitive to my shaking in terror. Much too quickly, in my opinion, and after giving me a thumbs-up, off we go like real surf pros, at least in Caleb's mind.

About fifteen seconds into it, a monster wave swallows me and spits me out near Caleb, causing him to fall off his board. He screams, which causes me to fall into a full-blown panic attack, snapping like a crocodile.

I definitely have no Lab characteristics so I cannot claim to be a natural-born swimmer, more like a natural-born sinker. I clamp down on Caleb's arm to save myself, causing him to scream even louder.

In my panic, I can't distinguish whether his screaming is because he's drowning or because blood oozes from his arm.

To make matters worse, a small shark appears out of nowhere heading straight for the bloodied waters surrounding us. I can't believe my eyes. Despite the chaos around me, I have the clarity of mind to remember that all those Hawaiian brochures claim there are no sharks within a hundred-mile radius of the beaches. I must be hallucinating, right? Well, apparently not, unless Caleb is having the same hallucination.

To his credit, and to my surprise, Caleb quickly regains his composure, grabs the end of his surfboard and with all his might, strikes the shark on the nose. Thankfully, the shark squeals like a pig and immediately changes direction. I don't remember much after that. I guess I succumb to shock.

The next thing I remember is Caleb being stitched up in the village hospital. What makes this story even more incredible is that to protect me from certain incarceration, Caleb lies to the medical staff saying his arm injury is from a shark bite. What a great Dad.

ON THE COUCH (Nagi):

Caleb has saved my life for a third time. I have to admit that when I heard the lie fall so easily from his lips (but he does get a lot of practice with Becca), I feel a lump in my throat. Is this what love is? Now I owe him. I guess I will have to follow through, after all, with my part in the plot to murder Mom.

ON THE COUCH (Caleb):

For some unexplained reason, my stomach isn't bothering me as much here. I guess being away from Becca, combined with all this healthy sunshine, clean air and outdoor exercise, has essentially relieved my stress. I now feel almost good as new and back to my old self.

CHAPTER EIGHTEEN

AFFAIR

Even though Rex is hanging out with me more and more, I continue to long for my own kind. I pray daily that God will smile upon me and send me a dog buddy. One day my prayers are unexpectedly answered.

My property is about five acres and completely fenced with squares large enough for a small animal to pass through. While I'm outside basking in the warm sun and contemplating my navel, my form of meditation on occasion, I naturally become quite drowsy. Just as my heavy eye-lids are about to drop, I'm startled by Tina Weiner. I've heard she's in the neighborhood and is prone to trespass whenever she has the chance.

Normally I would have sprung at her, always in attack mode like my wolf brothers, but she just looks so darn cute and innocent. Instead I stand up, walk over and wag my tail. She licks my nose before I have a chance to protest. From then on, I am silly putty in her paws. Have you ever heard of love at first smell?

Generally, I don't have much use for wiener dogs,

but Tina isn't like all the rest. She's a lady and humble in her mannerisms. Besides, she treats me like a Greek god, raving that I resemble Lassie with my classic profile. (Maybe Becca was right about Lassie taking over my body once it became pure). Tina goes on and on about how she loves my multi-colored coat and that every spot is a mystery she could spend hours contemplating.

Clearly, she's not just some superficial babe, but is 100% real. She's open, vulnerable, sensitive and responsive to my every thought. It's almost like she's inside my head. I think she can even taste my food without eating it. Oh, by the way, she doesn't like veggie glop any more than I do.

I just love it when she pees on everything I do… what a validation of my machismo. I love the way we bark in pitch at those pesky, annoying squirrels, and when we sniff each other… I have to tell you, two-leggers could market the fragrance as Parisian perfume.

Unfortunately, the odor doesn't last long, given the unnecessary bathing the two-leggers force us to endure. Don't they realize these baths cover and diminish our naturally alluring body odors?

Anyway, Tina and I grab time for our secret meetings whenever I can work it in around my co-therapy schedule. Often, we happily and lazily bask in the afternoon sun. Tina puts her little head on my belly and peacefully falls asleep.

I'm becoming so enamored with her that I can't stop thinking about her. I can easily forgo an entire week of meals, especially since they are glop-laden, to spend just five minutes with her.

ON THE COUCH (Nagi):

I hope Caleb isn't jealous. I know how he gets and how much he loves me, but I'm not giving up Tina Weiner. She understands me better than anyone, even Rex, who admittedly has offered worthwhile advice, now and then, through his creative and very bizarre story-telling.

Even so, the way I feel now, I could easily run away with Tina and never look back. My tics and biting are kicking in more because of my guilt. Sometimes I think I need to find a therapist. Oh wait, that's what I am, according to Dad. What's that old saying? Love is madness.

CHAPTER NINETEEN

TRAITOR

It's inevitable that Rex will discover my relationship with Tina Weiner sooner or later. Late one afternoon, when Tina has fallen asleep across my paws, Rex crawls up to my ear and screams loudly, "Up and at 'em!" We both jump as though shot from a cannon.

Tina's first reaction is to stomp Rex and eat him. I honestly almost let her, but decide against it, pulling her back before first chomp. Rex only makes a bad situation worse by saying, "Who's the new bitch?"

Before I can stop him from flapping his jaw any further, he begins his typical preposterous rhetoric.

"Let me introduce myself. I am Sir Rex Maxwellian and come from a long line of royal beetles. From the looks of you, sister, I take it there's no royal lineage running through those veins. You may have heard of King Tut? Well…"

I quickly interrupt him saying, "Oh please Rex, not this nonsense again."

"Hmmpph… nonsense??? Is that what you call it now, Nagi?"

Rather than responding to his ridiculous question, I make a proper introduction. "Rex, this is Tina Weiner, my neighbor."

"Yeah. Right. I can see she's *just* a neighbor. What's up with that? I thought I was the only one you felt that way about. You don't let me sleep in your paws."

"Now Rex, let's get real here. You're a beetle. Besides, in my sleepy stupor, I may mistake you for a flea and absent-mindedly nip at you, removing several of your handsome appendages, which would ruin your perfect form. You wouldn't want that, would you?"

Rex ignores me and focuses his attention on Tina.

"Well Teeny Weeny, if I may be so bold, let me tell you more about myself. Why I remember when Walt himself contacted me to play a part opposite Mickey. He was looking to create another larger-than-life character for the world to love - Barkley Beetle. There were no auditions because none were needed. Walt knew a good thing when he saw it. I would have gone on to super-stardom, had it not been for Stephen and Robert alerting Walt that I was a difficult study, couldn't follow directions, and was sue-happy. Believe me, those two career-killers haven't seen the last of me."

By now, I'm well aware that I must take it slow and be very careful in how I approach Rex to avoid his becoming testy and impulsive, so I softly toss out, "Rex, please stop."

As usual, Rex is on a roll and will not be deterred. "Well Teeny, I guess this is neither the time nor the place to go on and on about myself, but you need to know what you're up against. I'm his one true confidant, best friend and you will never replace me. I'm sure by now you know about his enslavement as co-therapist and his warped father's plans to kill his mother. He may be damaged goods, sister, but he's my damaged goods, got it?"

Then Rex, turning with teary eyes towards me, gulps and asks, "What does she have that I don't?"

"Rex, simmer down. You know I've always been faithful to you. You are my best friend and dare I say, consultant?"

"You're darn right, don't you ever forget it."

Before Rex can say anything else, Tina finally speaks up. "Rex, Barkley or whatever you think your name is at the moment, it's true that I love Nagi and that he confides in me, but if you are truly his friend and want to help him escape his life, we all have to work together as a team. And, in case your tiny pea-brain has forgotten, my name is Tina, not Teeny."

"Whoever," Rex mutters, turning his back and marching away in a huff.

ON THE COUCH (Rex):

Listen sister, I'll call you what I want. How dare you interfere and try to break my eternal bond with Nagi. Why, I remember my knighthood under King Arthur. At the Battle of Valegon, his sword slipped out of his hand and I retrieved it just in the nick of time. He continued the fight, which I'm glad to report, he ultimately won. He was so grateful for my saving his life that he carried me on his shoulders before thousands of soldiers and knighted me two days later.

I know who I am and nobody, I mean *n-o-b-o-d-y*, could ever replace me or have the depth of courage, wisdom, and yes, even intelligence to assist my buddy, Nagi, in coping with his dysfunctional life.

I'll try to be nice to Tea Cup, but only because I worry that Nagi will become angry or ignore me otherwise. God only knows how much he needs me.

Besides, maybe I'll come up with my own murder plot to do away with Teeny Weeny… Teeny Weeny… there I said it over and over… so take that, Teeny, you over-stuffed, over-inflated tootsie roll.

CHAPTER TWENTY

NEIGHBOR

One day as Tina Weiner and I lay soaking up some rays, Sugar Bear's name comes up out of the blue. Remember him? He's my misunderstood meathead neighbor, a big "tough" Rottweiler known for bullying all creatures, big and small.

Tina catches me up on all the neighborhood gossip, including her study of Sugar Bear, who she claims is highly entertaining, insisting that if his true character ever got out, his reputation would swiftly transform from neighborhood bully to local neurotic joke.

According to Tina, who has come to the conclusion that she knows as much about therapeutic diagnosis as I do, he has a classic case of Obsessive Compulsive Disorder (OCD). He begins eating after he circles his bowl exactly 10 times. Once he digs into his dry dog food, he counts out 10 pieces and drops them next to his bowl. He then carefully inspects each morsel, looks around to make sure no one is watching and then, quick as a viper, sucks up the morsels in one gigantic gulp. He never seems to chew.

He methodically does this repeatedly. Once he has vacuumed up the last 10 morsels, he licks the bowl precisely 10 times on the inside, before nudging it over the edge of the deck. The 30-minute ritual now complete, Sugar Bear lets out a deep thundering roar, after taking 10 shallow breaths.

Tina believes Sugar Bear is fixated on the number 10, but has not yet figured out the reason. She laughs at his compulsiveness. I don't laugh with her. Actually, I'm a little upset. The truth is that he's become one of my best buddies, and I don't appreciate others making fun of his idiosyncrasies.

Sugar Bear may have his odd behaviors, but who wouldn't, saddled with a name like that? Much as I love her, Tina could use some honest self-examination. She obviously has way too much time on her hands if she thinks she knows Sugar Bear so well, all without never having met him.

Sugar Bear's and my friendship comes about quite surprisingly one holiday weekend as we furiously bark and race along the fence that separates us. Sugar Bear suddenly stops mid-run, kicks the compacted dirt and snorts, baiting and challenging me.

Much as I try to do the same, my efforts are thwarted by the redwoods and I become entangled in the endless sprinkler lines Caleb has installed for hands-free watering. Sugar Bear plops down, rolls over on his back and laughs with gusto. For some unexplained reason, I follow suit. I must look pretty comical from his vantage point.

It's a definitive bonding moment that forever changes our relationship. We sit and have our first dog-to-dog conversation, during which he comes to understand my plight and I gain a clearer understanding of why he has developed OCD. (I guess it's pretty obvious. He's a big, thick Rottweiler cursed with that ridiculous name so he has an enormous need to over-compensate).

It's my fear of forgetting what a dog's life is truly like that prompts him to suggest a spontaneous adventure down the 3-mile dirt road near our homes. He helps me tunnel under the fence and we are off in no time.

It feels amazing to run free with no worries or obligations, with the wind blowing so fierce that my ears are pinned to my head. We are only gone for an hour or so, but during that time, we chase cats, bark at squirrels nestled safely on high tree limbs, and — ignoring the "No Trespassing" signs — race in tall grasses on undeveloped acreage. As usual, the stickers seem to jump out and attach to my thick fur but I don't care. I'm happy-go-lucky and living in the moment.

We chase cars and stand defiantly in front of nervous drivers trying to safely pass. We dig for gophers and tag-team a frightened wild hare, who thankfully escapes since we honestly don't know what we would have done if we had caught him. We even find a couple of horses to spook.

It's just a typical dog day afternoon and I'm loving life. For the first time in many years, I feel reconnected to my roots, to the nonsense that is my birthright.

The highlight of our great escape occurs when we cross paths with a fellow four-legger, attached to his parent by that confining rope they seem to love. We run towards them, barking wildly and circling. Much to our delight, the human shakes his fist at us, cursing. The dog jumps and twists, trying his best to escape, but he's hampered by that leash. In a feeble final effort to scare us off, his parent threatens to throw a rock at us. Such fun.

The danger of getting caught is intoxicating as we head home. As luck would have it, I return before I'm missed. Becca doesn't question all the stickers, patiently brushing them out, while mildly scolding me for traipsing in parts of the property not yet mowed.

This is one of my best days ever, but it makes me even more painfully aware of how far I've strayed from the normal life of a dog.

ON THE COUCH (Nagi):

To my surprise, Sugar Bear isn't the big bully he

pretends to be. He's just another poor misunderstood pooch. I truly learned a lot from him during our adventure. We even share an unexpected connection, that of being pound rescues. While caged in the pound prison for 10 days, waiting patiently for his original parents to retrieve him, he developed anxiety. Saddled with the name of Sugar Bear obviously threw him over the edge.

ON THE COUCH (Sugar Bear):

Nagi isn't so bad, after all. I hope we can plan regular short escapes together. Both of us definitely need playful distractions. As for Tina Weiner's uneducated observation, 10 is not an obsession but a comfort. I was born the 10th pup to a proud mama on the 10th day of the 10th month. My mama had exactly 10 black speckles dotting her white forehead, and a wet tongue that could give me a good cleaning in just 10 quick licks. So, 10 of anything always brings back tender memories of my first home and my mama's love.

CHAPTER TWENTY-ONE

THANKSGIVING

Every family has a loony relative or two, right? Well, Caleb is very close to one of his more dysfunctional siblings, his brother, Andrew. He and his wife, Kathryn, live about 100 miles away in the Lodi area. Every year, I am dragged along to Andrew's house for Thanksgiving. The worst part of it is being forced to socialize with the family mutts, snobs Roscoe and Lily.

On the ride over, Caleb gives me the same lecture: remain friendly, no fighting, no stealing food from the table, and absolutely no begging. Caleb calls it the Four Laws of Dog Civility.

Let me just say that from my training as Caleb's co-therapist, I have learned to refine my skills as a good judge of character, and Roscoe and Lily are the worst imaginable representatives of four-leggers. They are not only judgmental gossip mongrels, but aloof snits, as well.

Instead of the usual dog greeting, a tradition that is older than Sir Rex's fabricated royal lineage, Lily sticks her nose in the air and sashays right past me. When I attempt to greet Roscoe, he immediately lifts his back leg and just misses my front paws with his aim. He must think he has to defend his territory and prove his rank as Alpha male. Lily, like the true codependent that she is, always gives him a lick on his long, pointed nose in approval.

Roscoe is a German Shepherd, so he's not much bigger than me. I could take him, if I really want to, but I must follow the four laws set down by Caleb. In couples counseling, I would diagnose Roscoe as a narcissistic personality with aggressive tendencies and Lily, well she's a little prissy, phony twit with no depth and lots of issues. Nothing like my Tina Weiner.

Once, while trying to strike up a conversation, I asked her what she likes about living with her family and she replied: "I live in paradise. I love my special cookies, my ultra-comfy bed and thrive on the adoration of everyone who enters this household, present company excluded."

I can give you two more good reasons why I find these high-falutin' mutts deplorable.

Reason number one: they regularly set me up as the fall guy, and clearly ignore the Four Laws of Civility.

Let me explain. While Kathryn is making mashed potatoes for our Thanksgiving feast, she leaves the kitchen for a minute to run upstairs. Right there, in front of me and God, Roscoe seizes the opportunity, stretches to the counter top, and gulps half the lumpy taters. I'm so shocked that I just stand there in disbelief. Those few seconds give Roscoe all the time he needs to escape, leaving behind buttery droplets, and me as the obvious culprit when Kathryn returns.

Of course, she wastes no time complaining to Caleb and he wastes no time putting me out on the deck, chaining me up for the next three hours. I'm not even allowed inside during the big holiday feast, but have to watch through the large glass picture window as Roscoe and Lily blatantly beg for Thanksgiving hand-outs.

There they are enjoying my favorite morsels, while before me sits a bowl of boring dog food with a scoop of cold, bland mashed potatoes sitting on top. It's like looking at a bowl of food with white veggie glop. I even spot a couple of Roscoe's tell-tale hairs in the mix. Happy Thanksgiving to me.

The second reason occurs the following morning. After breakfast, the parents decide to take us all for a walk to the nearby park about a half-mile distance. I guess they think they need the exercise, after yesterday's gorging.

While the two-leggers marvel at a magnificent oak tree with a hawk nest, Lily quietly snaps at me and bites my back leg. Of course, I instinctively retaliate, growling like a banshee warrior and clamping down on her back leg.

The parents turn at that exact moment and gasp in horror. I release my grasp on Lily's leg, lower my head and cower much like a puppy caught with his paw in the biscuit jar. Again, guess who gets unfairly blamed? That's right. Me.

I'm marched back to the deck where Caleb scolds me, going on and on about my embarrassing behaviors. He then chains me up once again and there I sit for the next hour until the family returns from the park. I spend that hour fuming, pacing and planning for revenge.

My chance comes the next day, much sooner than I had hoped. Early in the evening, I overhear Kathryn bragging and showing off a cherished beaded evening bag that her great, great grandmother had left her. This is her pride and joy. I still can't figure out what the big deal is. It's really nothing much to bark about, especially given several loose, dangling threads and rows of missing beads.

As the evening winds down, we go through our normal doggie routines. Roscoe and Lily use the doggie door to go outside to do their business before settling in for the night. It's common knowledge that these two require at least two nightly trips outside due to their weak bladders. It's also common knowledge that I never need to go out after 9 p.m., always sleeping through the night.

But not tonight. About 2 a.m., I sneak out of Caleb and Becca's bedroom and tippy-paw down the carpeted stairs. I must confess that my creative genius still astounds me. This is how it all goes down.

Unfortunately for her, Kathryn has forgotten to place this precious item safely in the curio cabinet so I snatch the bag from the vanity, shred the material and beading to pieces, and then create a straight path leading to Roscoe and Lily's 14k gold-trimmed food bowls. To seal the deal, I even place a solitary bead in Roscoe's bowl.

I quietly return to the bedroom where my parents remain sound asleep. (Oh, by the way, I will have to let Caleb know that Becca's right. He's a real snorer.)

You would think my guilty conscience (and Caleb's snoring) would have kept me awake, but nope. Actually, I sleep better than I have in years until 7 a.m. when I'm sharply jolted awake by Kathryn's blood-curdling screams. Her attention seems to be focused on Roscoe and Lily. Oh, what satisfaction.

My heart beats so fast, I worry someone will surely notice and finger me as the true offender. This time, when Andrew again tries to pin the destruction on me, contrary to the evidence, my parents stand up for me, demanding that Roscoe and Lily be chained outside just as I have been twice before.

You know, life can be funny sometimes. When I was innocent, I was punished, yet when I was guilty, I walked away scot-free. Go figure.

For the remainder of the day and until we leave that night, Roscoe displays the utmost respect for me. However, Lily remains the snit that she is and will always be. What a bitch.

ON COUCH (Rex):

Nagi, what am I going to do with you? You finally redeem yourself at the end of your so-called vacation with those spoiled brats, but you sure took your sweet time about it. Why, I remember when I was special advisor to Abe Lincoln. Nobody knew that he consulted with me when he had an important decision to make and that I was really the beetle in charge of national defense.

Problems started when he stopped listening to me because of all the media hype. This was a huge mistake on his part. When tension built in the White House and in Congress between the Democrats and Republicans over his war decisions, I went directly to the president and pleaded with him to listen to me. Unfortunately for him, he pooh-pawed my advice.

My point is don't fear taking action against a power-ful president or two controlling ninnies like Roscoe and Lily. The sooner you claim your power, the better off you'll be. If you had put Roscoe and Lily in their places right from the beginning, you could have enjoyed your entire Thanksgiving holiday, instead of just a few hours at the end.

CHAPTER TWENTY-TWO

FAIRE

Every year, our small town holds a dog faire sponsored by the local SPCA as its main fundraiser. It's a combination of the Olympics, show-'n-tell, a carnival and a beauty contest, all rolled up into one huge fun day for me and my peers. Events are what you would typically expect at this type of function: newspaper fetch, musical chairs, best kiss and tail wag, pet and owner look-a-like, ball toss, top trick, and best costume.

Despite how entertaining and enticing it sounds, I have mixed feelings about attending. On the one paw, I can hang out with my own kind, make a few new friends, catch up on local gossip, and hopefully beg some tasty morsels from one of the many dog-lovin' vendors. On the other paw, if Caleb and Becca dress me up in some gaudy costume to parade me around again… well, that's just sideways.

As in previous years, both Caleb and Becca promise me they won't humiliate me by forcing me to participate, and, as in previous years, they break that promise.

Reluctantly, the only main event I agree to participate in is the paper fetch. Caleb practices with me for at least a month prior to the big day. Each morning, he rolls the newspaper, tosses it on the lawn, hoping and praying for my quick retrieval. Each morning, I watch in awe as he hurls the paper over and over past my nose. I never budge and he never stops throwing.

Let me explain my lack of interest with this newspaper thing. First, I hate the taste of ink. Second, only a goofus would mistake a newspaper for a ball.

Weary of Caleb's cajoling and bribing, we come to a quasi-understanding. I agree to fetch the paper in my own good time. Caleb is initially happy that I agree to budge, at all. However, in order to win the competition, Caleb insists that the newspaper be retrieved in less than 10 seconds. Considering my oppositional attitude, I usually stroll the indirect route, a quarter-mile out of my way.

That gives me a retrieval time somewhere between one minute and one hour, depending on my gait and any distractions I may encounter. In frustration, Caleb finally gives up and decides to leave my winning to fate.

The day of the faire arrives. The paper fetch is the third event so Caleb allows me to cruise the grounds to check out the other four-leggers. Unfortunately, I'm on a leash, which prevents my usual style of greeting.

I have never seen so many dogs in one place. As an experienced co-therapist, I immediately size them up. I have learned about non-verbal behaviors from Caleb and observing them provides me all the information I need to assess the character flaws.

It soon becomes obvious that there are many narcissistics like Roscoe, several codependents like Lily, a few histrionics and even some borderlines, who attempt to seduce any four-legger who moves… young or old, homely or handsome.

Watching the opening activities, we sit near a vendor offering prizes to any two-legger who successfully tosses a small dog cookie into plastic rings carefully lined in rows on a table top. Luckily for me, most of the participants are bad shots. Most cookies bounce off the table and into my waiting mouth. Even though all these goodies make me sluggish and sleepy, this could easily become my favorite event, and one in which I can finally be recognized for my true talents.

My enjoyment is cut short when the fetch competition is announced. As you may recall, I could have cared less about this event, much less winning it. This is payback; my chance to humiliate Caleb for a change.

I follow an Australian Shepherd who has retrieved the ball in seven seconds, the fastest yet. He obviously has no mind of his own, just empty space in that vacant head of his, totally controlled by the whims of his two-legger.

Okay, my turn. My leash is released. Ah, sweet freedom. Caleb tosses the paper about 50 feet from me. I sprint like a Kentucky thoroughbred, but my target isn't the newspaper. Instead, I take a right turn about 20 feet out and make a bee-line for this black Lab with gorgeous, intelligent eyes. I have been admiring her from a distance all morning. Honestly, the first time I laid eyes on her, I almost wet myself with excitement.

Anyway, I dart straight for her and lick her nose as an introduction and love gesture. Tina Weiner never enters my mind. Yes, I know… I'm such a dog. Before this magnificent specimen can respond and hopefully reciprocate my feelings, her owner jerks her back and Caleb is on me like bees-on-honey.

I hear the roar of laughter swell from the crowd and watch with delight as Caleb's face turns brighter than ketchup. Yep, karma's a bitch.

My taste of victory doesn't last long, however. I expected Caleb to enter me in the newspaper fetch. I didn't expect to be entered in the costume contest and musical chairs competition. These two events are sprung on me out of nowhere. Believe me, Caleb wastes no time getting his revenge in the costume contest.

This is, without a doubt, one of the worst experiences I've ever been through. As hard as it is for me to admit, I think Becca is actually a co-conspirator.

The brilliant idea is Caleb dressing up as Anthony and I, as Cleopatra. He places a black wig on my pointed head, a jeweled necklace around my furry neck, and a spaghetti-strapped dress around my muscular chest. Becca attempts to paint my cheeks with bright ruby-red lipstick. Caleb has to fight me on this, holding me down so I can't break away. I must look like a real tramp.

To make matters worse, a photo is taken in front of 75 or so spectators, all who seem to be pointing and laughing at me. I could have almost, I say, *a-l-m-o-s-t*, put up with this competition if I had been dressed like Batman or at least, if I could have played Anthony to Caleb's Cleopatra.

To really put the nail in the coffin, my latest love interest, the enticing Lab, witnesses this abomination. I think I spot a smirk cross her face as she sashays flirtingly past a flat-nosed, full-cheeked pug. Needless to say, Caleb and I place last.

You would think Becca might notice my pain and discomfort, and feel sorry for me, but no. To further humiliate me, I'm now faced with musical chairs. By now, all bets are off. I have no shame and throw caution to the wind.

Musical chairs is a simple game. There are 11 contestants but only 10 empty chairs and 10 rug mats. The music begins and we all circle the empty chairs and mats. The music stops and Becca dives for a chair, dragging me along, forcing me to sit next to her on the adjoining mat. At that point, the contestant standing is eliminated, along with one chair and one mat.

To my surprise, I actually enjoy this game, although the rules need to be modified. I'm really getting into the part of claiming my mat, my territory, especially since there is so little in my life that I have actual control over.

The music starts again, our cue to start moving… but I dig my paws in and don't budge. I'm changing the game rules. This small rug scrap is my new territory. I've earned it and am not about to give it up to that Queensland vying for my spot.

The music continues to play, with all competitors ignorantly continuing to follow the old rules, walking clumsily around Becca and me. If anyone comes within one foot of me and my mat, I bare my canines, growl, and lash out holding my ground.

All the while, Becca is unsuccessfully trying to cajole and drag me off the small rectangular rug. Suddenly the music stops and the announcer requests that Becca kindly leave the circle. It seems that the announcer doesn't understand or appreciate my rule changes and we are disqualified.

In disgrace, Becca drags me from the circle and away from the crowd, who seem, once again, to be laughing and pointing at me. But I'm not ashamed of my performance and prance off with head held high. A champion.

We find Caleb sitting under a shady oak tree laughing hysterically. "This is your fault, Caleb. You've finally succeeded in turning him into a neurotic mess. Proud of yourself?"

ON THE COUCH (Nagi):

I don't know about Caleb, but I'm especially proud of myself and my behavior today. I'm also proud of my parents. Dysfunctional as they are, they truly care about the plight of neglected, abused and discarded animals. They support the SPCA's efforts in educating the public about spaying and neutering as the only responsible way to stop the senseless destruction of so many unwanted four-leggers, who have done nothing wrong, other than being born.

Often, I overhear my parents discussing appalling story-after-story about dogs being thrown from moving vehicles, locked in closets with no food or water, abused, kicked and abandoned in the middle of nowhere. If dogs were the ones in power, we would never behave or treat others that way. The two-leggers could sure learn a few things from us. As crazy as my parents are, I know I'm loved, safe and secure, something very important to all living creatures.

ON THE COUCH (Rex):

Nagi told me the whole humorous story about that dog faire. I only wish he had taken me along for some coaching. Why I remember the time when I was assistant coach for the 1980 Olympic hockey winners. You think they won because of their talents? Or their coach? Nope. Let's give credit where credit is due. The victory was because of me.

Until now, no one knows that I crawled inside the opponent goalie's helmet. I waited patiently and when the puck was headed for the goal, I bit the goalie so hard that he couldn't concentrate on defending it. That's how the winning team beat the record for highest number of goals in a single game and became gold medal champions. I'm really the one who deserved the gold, not the players. I was the real talent but never received my deserved recognition.

If you had any sense, Nagi, you would have taken me along to help manage those crazy parents of yours. At the very least, I could have given Becca pointers on how best to dress you as an authentic Cleopatra. After all, let's not forget that my ancestors were her handmaidens. With my help, you just may have taken first place for best costume.

CHAPTER TWENTY-THREE

HALLOWEEN

Further humiliation looms. Caleb's office is planning the annual Halloween party. I've never been invited, but Caleb believes, now that I'm such a big part of his therapeutic strategies, that he would be remiss in not taking me… but as what?

The answer comes about quite naturally one day as Becca sings off-key, "Angel of Music" from "Phantom of the Opera."

Years ago, Becca had introduced Caleb to the beauty and passion of this hit musical, and he had become as big a fan as she, so the idea of my playing Christine to his Phantom became a no-brainer.

The problem is getting me to howl on cue. When Cabeb sings the lyrics "*…sing for me*," I am supposed to howl in higher and higher octaves until glass shatters. We never seem to get in sync, though. I don't know if it's my howling or his that makes us both off-key.

At any rate, it becomes evident very quickly that in order to enjoy our duet, spectators require thick and sturdy ear plugs. Mercifully, the party is postponed due to Caleb's sore throat.

ON THE COUCH (Rex):

How crazy is this guy? I've heard Nagi crooning and let me tell you, it ain't pretty. That Tea Cup is either tone deaf or madly in love.

CHAPTER TWENTY-FOUR

THERAPY

On one of those rare days when my parents are actually getting along, they leave me to my own devices. I invite Tina Weiner over for our sporadic ritual of comfortably lounging and lazing in the soothing mid-day sun.

Just as I'm about to doze off, perfectly content wasting my afternoon with Tina's sweet little head resting against my chest, Sugar Bear hollers over the fence, "Hey, Lover Boy. *Oh, Lover Boy.*" I don't appreciate his timing or his choice of words, so I think it best to ignore him in the hopes he will go away. No such luck. He persists in disturbing our peace. "Nagi has a girlfriend and they are *s-i-c-k-e-n-i-n-g.*"

Since it's obvious that we'll get no R&R today, Tina and I saunter over to the fence to see what's up with Sugar. On the way over, Tina reminds me that she doesn't really doesn't care for Sugar Bear and continues to find him and his OCD behaviors bizarre. I don't respond, believing her feelings are based on ignorance, and that once she gets to know him, she'll change her mind.

At the fence line, I tamely confront him with, "Hey, if I had a name like Sugar Bear, I wouldn't be teasing me about my love life." Sugar Bear, who can tell that I'm really not all that upset about it, grins and responds with "Touché." It seems that he just wants to get our attention to break up the monotony of his day.

We all settle down, with the fence between us. Being the lady she is, Tina does not show her dislike of Sugar or reluctance in sharing our afternoon with him. He comments on how calm and less stressed I seem today. I realize it's not only because I'm with Tina Weiner, but because my parents have been getting along so well lately.

It may have something to do with Caleb's chronic stomach pain, which seems to have taken a toll on his energy and quarrelling abilities. Out of necessity, he has had to depend upon Becca more and more. She actually seems to be enjoying her new role as caretaker, catering to Caleb's every desire and demand. At any rate, I plan on enjoying the peacefulness on the home front as long as it lasts.

With his usual flair, Rex pops in at that exact moment, halting all conversation. "Hey, what's up dogs? Why wasn't I invited to this little soirée? You know I'm welcome in the most intimate of circles, having acted with the A-list in Hollywood and served with presidents, yet you seem to exclude me at every turn. How quickly you seem to forget that I'm much more than a scarab beetle. Why, I served three years with President Nixon as his advisor on improving his political image. You've, no doubt, heard about that unfortunate incident involving water? I can't count how many times he called me late at night, waking me from one of my more vivid dreams of replacing him as president, to discuss how he should handle the media. Why I even sat in the tiny leather chair he had installed next to his diamond letter opener as he rehearsed his excuses to an unsuspecting America in defense of his secret election plot. So what's my point? If a US president seeks me out for advice and companionship, why not you three flea-bitten mutts?"

Tina and I pay little attention to Rex's ramblings, but notice that Sugar Bear hangs on his every word. "Wow, what a life you've had, Rex." Sugar seems to believe every lie that falls from Rex's lips. He also seems to have met Rex before, which is most likely the reason Rex doesn't descend into his classic spiel about his royal lineage. Honestly, I'm not sure what's going on here.

"Since we're all getting cozy, how about some group therapy? I *k-n-o-w* you all could benefit from it," remarks Rex. "Even though you're a co-therapist, Nagi, I have much more experience in facilitating this kind of thing, so I'll just take over, if you don't mind. I've learned from the best. You've heard of Sigmund Freud, right?

"Well, what you don't know is that I was his assistant and helped him develop Dream Interpretation, Free Association and the concept of the Oedipus Complex. I used to hang out in Sig's office, trying to learn and keep up with his latest therapeutic techniques.

"Now that he's gone, I was hanging out in a local therapy office, but ultimately determined that I had made a bad choice since the therapist seemed to be more confused than most of his clients. To entertain myself during his more mundane and robotic sessions, I usually skated down a make-shift ramp I improvised using a thick yellow pencil leaning against his coffee cup. Believe me, Freud, he's not."

For the first time since meeting him, Rex has my total attention. As I mentally relive my first encounter with him, things seem to suddenly fall into place. In my recurring dream during my pound imprisonment, it was Rex who was skating down that yellow pencil. How is it that I never made the connection until now? And, more importantly, how is it possible that I actually dreamt about Rex before ever actually meeting him? That would mean the bad therapeutic choice Rex refers to has to be Caleb.

"Since you claim to be familiar with Dream Interpretation, I have a puzzle for you, Rex. I first saw you years ago in my dreams. You were dressed as you are now and were skating down a yellow pencil, which was perched against a coffee cup on an office desk. I believe it was a therapist's office because there were two certificates on the wall, one with the word 'marriage' in it and the other with 'co-therapist.' I have so many questions. Why would I have such a clear dream about you when I've never in my life seen a creature remotely resembling you? And is Caleb the therapist you've been observing?"

"Great questions, Nagi. Let me try to explain in dog-ease language. In every dream, you either work out a present-day problem, resolve issues from the past or foretell the future. Your dream, Nagi, obviously falls into the latter category. It's clear that we share a very strong connection and were destined to come together. You also were destined to be adopted by Caleb and to become his co-therapist. Maybe it's so that you can intervene and prevent Becca's murder. As for observing Caleb in therapeutic action, well let's just say that I know more about him than I want to know. Enough said on that topic. Remember this is group therapy and it's not all about you, Nagi. Why don't we open the floor up to someone else?"

"But I'm the only one here with an immediate issue, Rex… as you all well know, I'm expected to participate in the murder of my Mom."

To pacify me, while at the same time trying to draw others in, Rex asks what they think. By their responses, evidently neither have been paying much attention.

"My name is Tina Weiner and I have a Napoleonic Complex." Unwilling to be left out, Sugar jumps in with "My name is Sugar Bear and I have OCD."

Rex, not big on self-diagnosis, thinks to himself that these two have been watching way too much television.

Rex claps two of his feet together. "OK, let's pay attention here, shall we? We're going to focus on Nagi. It's quite clear that you have mixed feelings, that you have loyalties to both your parents and that creates ambivalence. Tina, do you have any feedback?"

"Well, I think Nagi could possibly bite each parent to discover which one retaliates first; or maybe, he could have a little 'accident' on the carpet to find which parent becomes angrier. Then he'll know which parent loves him the most and he could then follow only that parent's directions."

"First, Teeny, you completely ignore Nagi's feelings and then you go directly to problem-solving," argues Rex. "That's not only against therapeutic rules, but it's also incredibly insensitive."

With that, Rex turns his back to Tina, giving Nagi a sly wink as if to say 'and you prefer her company to mine?' He then shifts his full attention to Sugar Bear, asking for his input.

"I think Nagi is feeling frustrated and guilty."

"Excellent… excellent," Rex says as he calmly reclines against a decorative, slightly chipped flower pot. "Please continue."

Feeling validated and impressed with his own observations, Sugar Bear delves deeper. "Well, I think Nagi shouldn't eat for three days to clear his body and mind. That's what I do when I find my OCD getting the better of me. I truly believe my parents give me chow containing too many preservatives and animal by-products. I've heard that can trigger…."

"OK… we've heard enough," interrupts Rex. "Once again, you have gotten off track and have lost focus so let me bring this session to some kind of conclusion. I have places to go and other critters to see. As I said earlier, Nagi, you love both your parents, are ambivalent, frustrated and feeling guilty, perhaps even some shame for your expected part in the murder plot.

"Why, I remember the time when Sigmund was dumbfounded as to what to do with a particular client, a woman who had disclosed that she intended to poison her husband. Sigmund was torn between his professional oath of confidentiality and wanting to prevent a murder. Naturally, being much more advanced intellectually, I developed a counter-plan, one in which Sigmund could both protect client confidentiality and foil the murder plot.

"What I did was sneak into the married couple's

bedroom the next night, bite the husband on his big toe so hard that he developed a nasty infection and had to be hospitalized for a few days. His wife felt so sorry for him that she completely dropped her plans to poison him. Once Freud understood what I had done, he coined the term 'displacement' and later received credit for an intervention that I obviously had developed."

"Talk about getting off-track," comments Sugar, barely holding back an exaggerated yawn. Mocking Rex further, he gently licks his paws while whispering, "I love me. Oh, how I love me. I'm wonderful." Mercifully Tina has dozed off and misses out on this spirited inter-action. Thus, our first-ever group therapy session comes to an abrupt halt, with nothing much accomplished. It reminds me of sessions with Caleb.

ON THE COUCH (Rex):

Wow, I really impressed myself today. Do those three realize just how lucky they are to benefit from my unparalleled wisdom, all free-of-charge?

ON THE COUCH (Sugar Bear):

I astonished myself with just how intuitive and connected I am. I must be a natural at this, a real wunderkind. Why, my therapeutic observations dance circles around Rex's opinions. Move aside, Freud, for the new generation of therapeutic genius. You're nothing but a has-been and your old side-kick, Rex, is as crazy as a bedbug… or should I say crazy as a beetle?

CHAPTER TWENTY-FIVE

AFRICA

Caleb has always wanted to take Becca to Africa. He had spent two years in Ghana, West Africa 20 years ago when he was in the Peace Corps and enjoyed the experience so much that he often remarks that nothing in his current life can ever compare to those carefree youthful days, when his life was filled with purpose and promise.

When Becca hears Caleb talk so passionately about Africa and how tedious his life is now in comparison, she often takes it personally, which usually leads to an argument.

One day in the heat of the moment, Caleb yells: "I'm tired of arguing with you, Becca. I'm going to Africa with Nagi and, by the way, you're not invited."

Caleb wastes no time in planning the very expensive two-week trip.

Becca couldn't have cared less about tagging along on Caleb's nostalgic whimsy. She is, however, extremely upset about Caleb spending $5,000 to daytrip down memory lane, especially since she has returned the diamond "Marilyn" ring that Caleb ranted about being too pricey.

Becca is also worried that Caleb will be poison-free for two weeks, which could possibly diminish the damage she has already inflicted on Caleb's body, and thereby reduce his need for her.

As for me, I'm honestly enthused about seeing Africa because I believe I will finally find my roots. I've heard that everybody finds their roots in Africa, so why not me? Someone once said I resemble an African Basenji. I'll need to check out those wild four-legger ancestors for myself. If my search is successful, Caleb may be returning home to Becca… solo.

The 14-hour plane trip is exhausting. Of course, I'm not given a first-class or even a second-class seat. Despite Caleb's urgings that I'm actually a seeing-eye dog, I'm crammed in a wooden crate stored below in freight. If not for Rex stowing away in my fanny pack, I don't think I could have survived being labeled as "luggage."

Rex and I entertain ourselves by making plans for the Serengeti, but before I can finish expressing my excitement to Rex about the prospect of finding my roots, he interrupts, as usual.

"Speaking of roots, I come from a long line of scarab beetles… going all the way back to the days of the pharaohs. Did you know that my father actually sat beside King Tut and acted as his advisor?"

"Shut up, Rex, you've already told me about your roots. Believe it or not, everything isn't always about you. What about my roots?"

"Let's finish talking about me first, Big Boy, shall we? I've never told you about my mum's side of the family."

I remain silent, studying a piece of luggage that reeks of rotting cheese. My stomach instinctively responds, growling in hunger.

"How can I say this? I guess the best way is to just blurt it out," Rex continues. "My great grandmother, 10 times removed (Chaka), did not come from superior scarab linage… she was actually an Aztec dung beetle. Her great grandparents immigrated to Egypt from Mexico in search of a better life."

"Isn't a dung beetle lower on the food chain than a sow bug?"

"Hey, that's my flesh and blood you're slamming. Anyway, even though she was not of noble blood, when Nero, my great grandfather 10 times removed, spotted her hunched over, struggling to carry heavy pieces of dung on her back to seal the cracks in the Giza pyramid, he pitied her, summoning her to the royal household.

"He told Tut that despite her stench, there was

something singularly beautiful about her crooked little smile and humped back. Because Nero considered himself blessed to act as advisor to Tut, he had vowed earlier that Spring to pay it forward, which, in his mind, meant saving this miserable creature from her obviously wretched existence.

"To make a very long romantic tale a little shorter, not only did Nero save Chaka, he married her. The Pharaoh, so moved by Nero's selfless and loving gesture, decreed that from that day forward all dung beetles would be equal to scarab beetles and would never have to carry dung again." Rex falls flat on his back, which typically indicates that he has completed his tale.

"I always thought I smelled something peculiar about you, Rex. No wonder you're so preoccupied and attracted to garbage cans. Now that I think about it, the dung in you is pretty transparent."

Rex is already lightly snoring. Since there's no point in pursuing any further dialogue, I follow suit and curl up to sleep the rest of the trip. Maybe napping will make the time go quicker.

When we touch down in Accra, the capital of Ghana, the stifling heat is suffocating. I want to do nothing but lounge in front of an air conditioner or cool down in a pool of clear water.

The heat doesn't seem to bother Caleb, but then he's

not wearing a thick white fur sweater like I am. He's quite happy, almost giddy out in the blistering sun as we commute to nearby towns and villages that Caleb had once visited.

Unfortunately, everything has changed dramatically. Worse yet, Caleb is informed that his Ghanian counterpart and guide, Kwame, had died just two months earlier. Caleb had planned to spend several days with his old friend, a man he had spent two years working beside; a mentor he greatly admired and respected.

Caleb becomes lethargic and aimless, obviously very upset by the news, which seems to temporarily put a damper on any possibility of fun for me and Rex.

By now, much as I hate to admit it, I'm a committed co-therapist and helping my Dad work through his grief and loss becomes my priority. Out of necessity, I'm there for him and respond to his every beck and call. No matter how silly the request. Everything he says I agree with, everything he wants me to fetch, I'm Johnny on the Spot. I even let him hold me next to him while he naps. Sometimes he squeezes me so hard I pass gas, but he never seems to notice.

By the third day, I have fully 'healed' him and we are off for more adventures, his more than mine. It seems that Caleb has a keen desire to revisit many of the places he hung-out at decades ago. He rents a jeep and drags me along, pointing out buildings, villages, markets or bars. I can see that he loves this trip down memory lane and so I put up with it, even though I'm mentally elsewhere.

What I am waiting for and what Caleb has promised me is a safari in the big game parks, Amboseli or Serengeti. Ever since I found out I would be visiting Africa, I've had this fantasy about a family of welcoming Basenjis accepting me into their pack.

However, as the first week of our vacation comes to a close, Caleb spends most of his time at the Peace Corps headquarters bragging about himself and his ancient African accomplishments to naive young volunteers who seem to appreciate his stories, hanging on to his every fabricated and exaggerated word. Still, I remain patient, hopeful my time for fun and adventure will come soon.

My patience pays off when we fly to Nairobi, Kenya the next morning. Caleb rents a Range Rover and we head toward Amboseli on a particularly sticky, hot summer day. The animals must have taken refuge from the heat, because they are nowhere to be found.

Hour after hour, we drive deeper into the game park and the only animals I see are vultures circling our vehicle. Quite honestly, I find this whole experience pretty disappointing.

To break the monotony of driving along the dusty

road, I request a much-needed potty break near a watering hole. After relieving myself, I decide to gulp down
some cooling waters. That's when I spot the baby rhino,
barely hidden by the savannah grasses. I'm in awe of
his size and uniqueness. He reminds me of a misshapen
unicorn. Rex finds nothing appealing about this baby,
however, and seizes the opportunity to toss out an
insult. "Hey, you over there. The ugly one. Yes, you.
Where did you get that big wart on your head?"

The baby looks at his reflection in the watering hole
and a tear slowly falls down his cheek as he makes a piti-
ful moan. Rex finds his comment thoroughly entertaining and howls at his unbridled wit. That's when Mom
makes her appearance, protecting baby and charging us.

We run to the vehicle and Caleb attempts to throw
it in gear. He isn't quick enough, though, as Mom rams
our jeep several times before it can muster up enough
speed to pull away.

Just as I begin releasing a sigh of relief, unbelievably
Rex jumps on Mom's horn, screaming "Yee hah, ride-em
cowboy" as though he's performing at the town rodeo.
Mom goes berserk, trying to buck him, but Rex seems
glued to her horn and hangs on.

Knowing something has to happen, but not sure
what that something is, and without much thought, I
jump on Mommy rhino's back to try to rescue Rex. This
infuriates Mom even more and she unpredictably stops

mid-run. Her braking causes Rex and me to fly about 50 feet in the air, landing smack-dab in front of Caleb, who is more than a little shaken up.

As Mom returns to her whimpering baby, Caleb gives me a tongue-lashing, while Rex chuckles sheepishly, well-hidden in my ear.

Because of this incident, Caleb decides it best that we lay low and rest the next day, that it's important to stay out of any potential trouble and take it easy before heading back to the states.

Since we didn't spot any African exotics while traversing Amboseli, other than the rhinos and vultures, Caleb thinks the next best thing is a trip to the Nairobi Animal Nursery for an up-close and personal view of chimps, lions, gorillas, giraffes and elephants. He also figures it's a safe environment, where nothing out of the ordinary can occur. He obviously has neglected to enter Rex into the equation.

The nursery is amazing. There are babies of every species, of every shape, size and color. Some are cuter than others and the baby wildebeest is quite a sight. I'm really not sure how to describe her, but the old adage, "She's so ugly that she's cute" seems to fit. The best part of the experience is that there are no anxious mothers charging after curious onlookers.

To my surprise, Rex is actually behaving himself and

seems to be enjoying the little ones. He's especially taken with the two-month-old giraffe, Geoffrey. Rex studies his every move and reads Geoffrey's stats several times: weight of 70 pounds; height: 4 feet; neck length: 2 feet.

As Caleb and I leisurely stroll towards the direction of a softly meowing baby lion, I turn to notice some commotion back in Geoffrey's pen. An astonished crowd has gathered, pointing towards the baby. That's when I notice Rex is no longer dangling from my collar. Worriedly, I correctly assume that Rex is the reason the crowd has gathered.

I race back to Geoffrey's pen to see what's-what. There in all his glory, I spot Rex slipping and sliding down Geoffrey's slim and trembling neck. The more Geoffrey pants and trembles, the more Rex enjoys the ride. It's fascinating, actually, much like studying a surfer expertly maneuver an unpredictable wave.

Thankfully, before I can think of a way out of this, Rex makes his ride short and triple flips off the top of Geoffrey's head, making the perfect landing on the top of mine.

The crowd is animated in their disapproval and they circle us (much like the vultures), but my sure-footed-ness and speed allow for a narrow escape. I'm grateful that we leave Africa without further incident, but am quite tired of coming to Rex's rescue.

Sometimes I honestly think he's just trying to collect more stories for future embellishment.

ON THE COUCH (Nagi):

I have put up with your grandiose delusions, your lies, and even your put-downs to my one true love, Tina Weiner, but your antics today were dangerous, Rex. I'm truly at a loss as to why you do the things you do, other than having another story to exaggerate when bragging about your improbable escapades.

ON THE COUCH (Rex):

Lighten up, you sissy. I was just trying to put a little fun in this dreary African safari. You and Caleb are so humdrum. As for that Mommy rhino, she's my old buddy, Roxie. We go way back, and Ride 'em Cowboys is our favorite game. Her baby, who I not only helped name, but assisted in the birthing of, is Joey and he obviously needs a little toughening up if he's going to make it in the African wild. He's almost as big a sissy as you are, Nagi.

ON THE COUCH (Caleb):

I feel much healthier in Africa and am sleeping better than ever. This only confirms my conviction that life with Becca is detrimental to my mental, emotional and physical health.

CHAPTER TWENTY-SIX

SIDEWAYS

I'm surprised I can sleep at all, especially since tomorrow is "D" (death) day for Becca. Sideways visits me again in my dreams. This time, while meditating on the front lawn and trying to erase tomorrow's events from my consciousness, I hear that high-pitched, squawky voice. I'd like to think that I've made contact with my inner spiritual guide, but deep down, I know the truth. There's no way my inner guide would sound like this.

"Hey Nagi. Got it yet?" About 20 feet up, in a near-perfect straight line above me, sits Sideways. Instead of the penguin suit, he now wears what looks like cowboy spats, a fringed vest, and a blindingly-white cowboy hat perched cockeyed atop his head.

At that moment, I think to myself that I really need to give up this meditation thing if Sideways represents my inner voice. Surely, I can do better than an out-of-shape squirrel with questionable fashion sense.

As my thought-pattern wanders in no particular

direction, out of the blue, Sideways transforms into a huge jet-black raging bull. Hot steam flows freely from its nostrils as its hoofs angrily claw the ground, preparing to charge. I begin to run, but fall. The bull falls or jumps, I'm not sure which, on top of me.

Petrified and immobile, I play dead. Out of the blue, this clumsy animal licks my face affectionately, briefly transforming into Becca. She whispers in my ear, "Follow your heart, Nagi. I know you'll do the right thing."

I gasp, trying to catch my breath. When I open my eyes again, Sideways is crouched beside me, crunching contently on a large oak nut, covered with chocolate. His image fades, while his words linger. "Remember, Nagi. Be true to yourself. You can't go wrong if you listen to your heart. Now, breathe… breathe… breathe…"

ON THE COUCH (Rex):

Who does this Sideways think he is? And how dare he traipse around in my territory for the second time now. If Sideways sneaks into my dreams, I'll show him what's what and who's who, even though I do understand what he's trying to accomplish with Nagi. I only hope that Nagi can start analyzing and taking his dreams more seriously. I always have and look where it's got me.

Why, I remember one of my more significant dreams, the details of which are not important. What is important is that I understood my dream's message and was able to reach General George Patton in the nick of time, thereby preventing an unnecessary and particularly brutal battle in North Africa.

ON THE COUCH (Sideways):

Why can't Nagi understand that I'm his higher self, looking out for what's best for him? With the pending harmful events in his life, he needs to stop these foot-dragging, lolly-gagging behaviors, snap to and get on the right track *NOW*. Time's a-wastin'.

CHAPTER TWENTY-SEVEN

DEATH

Caleb begins marking the countdown. In one month, he will be free of Becca and soon after, Gilbertoh.

I actually love Becca and am becoming more and more obsessed on finding a way out of this ill-fated plan. Caleb reassures me, and himself, that he has thought of everything and that, once we have waited the socially appropriate mourning period, we will take the insurance money, serve Gilbertoh to the cops as the fall-guy, and set up shop on some exotic Caribbean island. He promises I will then experience a feast of meaty delights daily, so much so that it will erase all those torturous years of veggie glop. As tempting as this is, I remain opposed to his plan.

The fateful day finally arrives. At the office, Caleb spends every spare moment going over what the plan is for that night. He surprises me by continually commenting, "I know this is going to be hard for both of us. I hope we don't chicken out." This gives me a flicker of false hope that Caleb will back out at the last minute.

As intended, Caleb is especially attentive to Becca's every need that evening. No want is too big, no demand unreasonable. Caleb even nibbles on her ear as he draws her a warm bath filled with luxurious bubbles. That's sideways. Sideways! That makes me think of my dream just the other night, the one where Becca told me to listen to my heart, to do the right thing. Well I don't need to listen to my heart when my head is screaming. I know what's right and helping Caleb isn't it.

Fear settles in. I just don't know if Caleb will make good on his threats if I don't participate. But what will happen to us both if I do? I hang around Caleb in a state of confusion. He, of course, is preoccupied with ensuring his plan falls perfectly into place.

Just as Caleb anticipated, the warm water, combined with the half-bottle of red wine she had consumed over dinner, makes Becca feel secure and loved, and she becomes putty in his hands. It's almost as though she is going along unwittingly with her part in the murder plot, too.

We all hit the sack at about 10 p.m. What a ridiculous pretense, like Cabeb or I can sleep. At exactly 12:30 a.m., I act my part, barking incessantly as though there is a bear in the house ready to attack.

This isn't exactly how the plan is supposed to go, but I ad lib in the hopes that Caleb will be forced to give up on this madness. However, Caleb jumps out of bed, which awakens a dazed Becca. "What's going on?," she mumbles. Caleb whispers, "I think there's a burglar in the house, in the entry way. I'm going to the garage to get my gun. Stay here, and be very quiet, my love." He even takes the time to give Becca a quick peck on her forehead.

While Caleb retrieves the gun, I continue to do my part haphazardly and nudge the chair down the center of the hallway. This is the most important part of his plan because Caleb can then claim that Becca, in her panic to escape, tripped over the chair.

I hear Caleb cry out, "Becca, get out of the bedroom now, the burglar has a gun and is heading in your direction." Trusting Caleb's words and without hesitation, Becca runs down the hall, which has been purposely darkened. I hear Becca trip or bump into the chair causing it to slide and screech across the hardwood floor.

Caleb now has her exact location. I keep my paws crossed that Caleb will change his mind at the last minute and settle on divorce instead. What I hear next is the deafening sound of the .45 followed by the unmistakable thud of Becca hitting the floor.

Oh my gosh, he actually followed through with it. I'm in a state of disbelief as I run towards Becca, my eyes full of tears. I gasp for air in a feeble attempt to fight off a full-blown panic attack.

Caleb gets to Becca first and cradles her in his arms. With what looks like a lopsided half-grin, Becca whispers in Caleb's ear, "I'm so sorry, Caleb… for poisoning you. I was only trying to bring us closer and really didn't want to hurt you. The rat poison is behind the water heater in the garage. I'll always love…"

And then, in what seems like a split second, Becca takes her last breath just as Caleb lets loose with a blood-curdling, gut-wrenching scream. At this point, I'm not sure who he's performing for and run outside to hide both my crushing pain over losing my Mom and my escalating anguish over Caleb taking her from me.

Caleb, like a finely-tuned killing machine, easily switches to the next phase of his plan, calling 9-1-1 and posing as the grief-stricken husband. Within 15 minutes, there's a knock at the door. Caleb allows sheriff investigators to inspect the crime scene, answering all their questions and pointing the finger at Gilbertoh between stifled sobs and erratic rocking motions.

He is barely able to choke out the details of Gilbertoh's intimidating office visit several months earlier and the ensuing threatening phone calls, eluding that the locket is the true motive behind the break-in and murder.

As it turns out, Caleb is quite the actor and Sheriff Danworth takes it all in, seemingly believing every lie that spews out of Caleb's mouth. However, I'm still not quite sure Caleb's version of a botched burglary is a sale, especially since there are no signs of forced entry. Besides, everyone knows that all the television detectives suspect the spouse first, right?

The investigative squad takes the next two hours to snoop, dust for prints, examine door locks and windows, and hunt for any other possible forensic evidence. And then Becca is gone forever. Just like that the coroner zips her in a big black bag and places her in the back of a hearse. For me, it seems like Becca is hauled away, much like taking out the trash.

I remain outside during the whole ordeal. The authorities continue their interrogation for the next couple of days. Of course, Caleb is well-rehearsed and prepared for all their questions. He's advised not to leave town, just as a matter of formality, insists Sheriff Danworth.

On the surface, it appears Caleb has gotten away with my Mom's murder.

ON THE COUCH (Caleb):

I can't believe it. After the sheriff and coroner left, I looked behind the water heater and found a half-filled box of rat poison, just like Becca said I would. It explains all my stomach pains, nervousness and insomnia these past several months, and more importantly,

why I always felt better during my vacations away from
her. In hindsight, it's probably a good thing I did Becca
in before she caused me serious and irreparable body
damage.

ON THE COUCH (Nagi):

I discover later that Caleb's scream was not for
Becca, but for himself. He's even stooped so low as
to give me some song-and-dance story about Becca's
deathbed confession, in which she supposedly added
rat poison to his veggie glop tester. As proof, he says
he found the half-empty box behind the water heater.
With that, Caleb puffs up his chest, parading around
like a peacock, apparently proud that he beat Becca to
the punch. I'm not buying it, though. I think Caleb is
concocting justification for murdering my Mom.

ON THE COUCH (Rex):

Nagi, how can you sleep at night, knowing what
you know? If you don't do something, I will. Remember
when we had that long talk about speaking from your
heart? You will never be able to live with yourself if you
do not tell the truth about Becca.

Why, I remember when I was working for the
FBI and my partner, Agent Elliot Ness, attempted a
cover-up. He had information as to where the notorious

Baby Face Nelson was holed up. It was common knowledge that Baby Face planned on blowing up the Capital building in DC. Somehow, don't ask me how or why, Baby Face paid Elliot to keep quiet.

Well, I had to speak from my heart and ratted out my partner, which was an extremely difficult thing to do. We had been together for more than 20 years. I was really torn up about turning in someone I loved, but guess what? I never felt as proud of myself as I did that day when Elliot was sentenced to 25 years in prison for fraternizing with the enemy. I received a Purple Heart for saving the lives of hundreds of DC politicians. You won't receive a Purple Heart for ratting out your Dad, but your conscience will be clear and you'll sleep better at night, just knowing that you did the right thing.

ON THE COUCH (Sheriff Danworth):

Normally, I would be initially suspicious of the spouse in a case like this, but Caleb seems to be a real stand-up guy. I've been doing this a long time and my gut tells me that we need to find this Gilbertoh character before he can cause any further harm to Caleb. From the looks of that dog of his, Caleb is pretty much on his own as far as protection goes.

ON THE COUCH (Nagi):

Got that right.

CHAPTER TWENTY-EIGHT

ADIOS

Despite Sheriff Danworth's edict to stay put, Caleb decides that a quick trip is warranted, given that the blood-stained carpet is a steady reminder of what had transpired less than a week ago. He also has a hard time seeing me mope around the house in a constant state of depression and anxiety, so Caleb plans an impromptu trip to Mexico. He figures we'll be back in town before the authorities even know we're gone so it will have to be a speedy there and back kind-of-thing.

Because we can lounge at the Pacific Ocean anytime here in the states, Caleb thinks a trip to the interior may prove more interesting so Mexico City becomes our destination.

This idea completely surprises me, given our last meeting with Gilbertoh. However, Caleb seems to be mighty impressed and proud of himself these days, strutting around with an air of invincibility.

We stay in a popular hotel in the Zona Rosa, which apparently isn't the safest or quietest area due to the night air filled with piercing elongated screams, repetitive gunshot pops and whirling police sirens.

Despite our sleepless nights, we enjoy days filled with mindless sightseeing. We visit Chapultepec Castle, a must-see for first-time visitors. We ride the carousel in the park, all in all a very relaxing trip if it weren't for my gnawing guilt.

The morning we are to leave, we stroll along downtown blocks to kill some time. To our surprise, right there, in the middle of the street is an enormous hole, with nervous excavators and excited archaeologists chattering and running about. As the story goes, a few months earlier, an ancient burial site had been discovered at this exact spot and the government is funding further exploration.

For a minimal fee, the public is allowed to climb down a few short steps below street level, to take a tour. Caleb shells out the pesos and we head underground.

There really isn't much to see, other than a large altar, apparently for sacrifices, and what looks like a mummy's encasement over in one corner. I would have said that Caleb had wasted his pesos if it hadn't been for the engravings on the tomb. Embossed in brilliant gold is the image of a large beetle. Beneath the image is written: *Aztec Dung Beetle, Chaka, wife to Scarab Beetle Nero, advisor to King Tut, and great grandmother (10 times removed) to Sir Rex Maxwellian.*

I stand dumbfounded. Can it be possible that Rex has been telling the truth all this time? His stories are just so impossible to believe. I can't wait to get back to talk to him about it. Hard to believe, but I miss the little guy.

We return to our hotel, pick up our luggage and hail a cab to take us to the airport. Mexico's cabbies are infamously notorious bad drivers, and our cabbie lives up to the reputation. He not only speeds along the crowded highways, but is very erratic, making unexpected turns at the last minute. We discover why when bullets whiz by, shooting out the side windows.

One of the bullets hits our driver in the shoulder, causing the cab to veer off the road and into a ditch. Before we have time to get our doors open, machine guns are shoved in our faces.

The cab driver and one of the bad guys, who I now recognize as Gilbertoh, are arguing in Spanish so we can't understand what's going on. Actions transcend language barriers, though, and without hesitation, Gilbertoh's buddy steps in, obviously having had enough useless conversation, waving his semi-automatic in the cabbie's nose. He gets the message loud and clear, running off down the road, leaving Caleb and me to fend for ourselves.

I'm scared spitless. Caleb and I are blindfolded and roughly yanked into a white, non-descript van with no license plates. It appears Caleb's time is up, that Gilbertoh has run out of patience waiting for the delivery of the locket or the cash.

Despite my terror, I have the sense to realize that Caleb's carelessness and devil-may-care attitude may have cost us our lives.

We are taken to a large hacienda on the outskirts of Guadalajara. It is remote and well-guarded, so any screams for help prove futile. Once we are settled and tied down, Caleb seems to gather his wits and attempts to communicate calmly with Gilbertoh, while I'm drawn to tantalizing, sweet smells from the kitchen. My body instinctively takes over, my nostrils breathing in deeply as my stomach growls involuntarily.

Caleb has other immediate problems to contend with. By now, I know him so well that I can almost see the wheels spinning in his head as he tries to come up with a rational way out of this, all to no avail.

So far, the only thing he has managed to accomplish is to annoy and agitate our captors, who have warned him more than once to keep his mouth shut or he will no longer have a tongue with which to speak.

I'm really not sure where Caleb's bravery suddenly emerges from. Perhaps, now that he is a seasoned killer, he can easily vacillate between scared spitless and daring fearlessness, and can actually enjoy this dangerous game of "cat and mouse."

I go unnoticed in the corner of the room, which is just fine with me and my stomach. My hope is that Caleb will continue to distract them with his lunacy, while I attempt to chew through my ropes and perhaps indulge in a little self-biting to calm myself... maybe even sneak a peek in the kitchen. I really have no escape plan past this.

Focused completely on my chewing, my ears perk up when I overhear Caleb talking about Becca and her untimely demise. This makes me pause so I can concentrate on what Caleb is actually saying to our captors.

Clever Caleb offers a proposal. In exchange for our release, Gilbertoh will receive half of the pending insurance monies, $500,000. Should Caleb renege on this promise, Gilbertoh will have his written and signed confession to Becca's murder, which he can then forward to Sheriff Danworth.

Gilbertoh gives Caleb a sinister grin, as if to say something far worse will occur should Caleb not follow-through. Ignoring Gilbertoh's obvious contempt, and flashing his most engaging smile, Caleb insists it's a win-win.

Luckily for Caleb, Gilbertoh is blissfully unaware that he is currently the prime suspect in Becca's murder. Had he known, I suspect that his rage and retaliation would have been quite swift and deadly, for both of us.

After several tense and silent seconds, Gilbertoh whispers in a corner with his comrades, who demand some kind of proof. Casually shrugging, Caleb removes a small piece of torn newspaper from his wallet, the obituary giving pertinent personal information on Becca, including her date of death and next of kin.

Even so, this is not an easy decision for Gilbertoh. It seems as though he would rather forego the cash to have his torturous way with Caleb. However, upon the urging of his fellow thugs, Gilbertoh reluctantly concedes, setting pen and paper before Caleb. I'm grateful it works out this way, especially since my jaw is getting a little sore from all my unsuccessful rope gnawing.

Once Caleb has signed his confession, we are whisked to the airport and are on way back home to bide our time before collecting the insurance money.

Caleb gives himself a huge pat on the back for his quick thinking with our captors. He's also proud of himself for getting away with the perfect murder. It wasn't as difficult as he had thought it would be. He's more surprised than I that he is able to sleep like a baby, and with a clear conscience. In his mind, he won his demented race with death.

ON THE COUCH (Rex):

I'm so disappointed with Nagi. I don't even want

to see his face. That's why I passed on the Mexico trip. Besides, it also gives me more alone time with Tina Weiner to catch her up on my fascinating adventures and to plot a plan to persuade Nagi to snitch on Caleb.

ON THE COUCH (Tina Weiner):

Rex is driving me crazy. He has not given me one moment's peace since Nagi has been gone. If I have to sit through one more of his fantastical stories, I will have no choice but to use him as a not-so-tasty appetizer. How on earth does Nagi put up with his narcissism?

Rex is right about one thing, though, and that is something has to be done about Caleb.

ON THE COUCH (Nagi):

Despite my near-death experience in Mexico, my thoughts are mainly on Rex. To think that all his mad ramblings have some semblance of truth is quite fascinating to a co-therapist of my stature.

As for Caleb, I'm grateful for his quick thinking, but really don't know how he can live with what he has done to Becca. It's time I use my therapeutic skills to evaluate Caleb's mental state, especially since his dark side seems to have emerged with a vengeance. I know he has been depressed at times, but after this Mexico trip, I now see his more manic side.

During captivity, he became so impulsive, grandiose and was talking so fast (pressured speech) that I could barely understand him. It now makes more sense as to why Becca complained about Caleb not sleeping for days, even though he insists it was due to the gradual poisoning, which, by the way, I still don't believe.

My keen discernment and analytical skills tell me that Caleb's diagnosis is bi-polar, anti-social personality disorder with narcissistic features. If I share this diagnosis with Caleb, he will, no doubt, blame his mother for any and all psychological defects.

I wonder if Caleb will ever own up to his negative behaviors, serious mental disorders and treachery against Becca, the only human who truly understood and cared about him.

ON THE COUCH (Gilbertoh):

Wow, what a scary bunch I associate with. I don't know how much longer I can fool them. As for Caleb, even though I'd much rather have my family recipe, a half-million dollars will not only pay for culinary school, but help finance my future restaurant. The deadline for school registration is in three months, so he'd better hurry with that insurance money.

CHAPTER TWENTY-NINE

ARRESTED

Caleb's right. The authorities never discover we had left town. They were apparently too busy wrapping up the case.

In the meantime, Caleb goes on with life. Now that Becca is no longer around, there's no reason for Caleb to protect me, and therefore, no need for me to co-counsel with him.

Being left at home gives me time to think. As much as I had initially wanted to discuss my findings in Mexico with Rex, I find myself consumed with Becca. I don't know how Caleb can live with what he has done. Even though I played a very minor part in Becca's demise, I don't know how I can live with myself either.

Days turn into weeks and weeks into months. Caleb laughs often, throws my balls in an attempt to engage me, and incredibly seems more at peace since he has the house to himself.

The only monkey wrench is the weekly calls from Gilbertoh to check-in on the status of the promised cash pay-off. Sometimes, I wish I possessed my Dad's callousness and guilt-free conscience.

It doesn't take long for Caleb to effortlessly rid himself of every reminder of Becca. Every single piece of clothing, artwork, books, and furniture that Becca claimed as her own is gone. He also trashes every photograph of her.

This is the final straw. I know I must tell the truth. It's the only way I can move on, no matter what the consequences may be. Little does Caleb know that I have kept the notes he made during our camping trip, three very-legible pages with five promising ideas to take Becca out.

In my wildest dreams, I never thought I would have to use this against him because I never believed he would go through with murdering my Mom, but now, his smugness and air of conceit are infuriating.

Caleb bides his time waiting for the insurance cash and I bide my time waiting for final news from the authorities.

About 30 days later, Sheriff Danworth comes to the house to inform Caleb that the investigation is temporarily shelved, while they work out some kind of deal with the Mexican authorities.

Even though I know it's now or never, I remain glued to my spot for some unexplained reason and watch paralyzed as Caleb walks the sheriff to his car, amicably chatting all the while about being available for any further assistance he can provide to help solve the case and bring Gilbertoh to justice.

He, of course, really doesn't want the authorities to find Gilbertoh, but should this happen, he prays crazy Gilbertoh will go down fighting and be killed in the shoot-out.

The sheriff, who seems sucked in by Caleb's nonchalance and charm, takes the opportunity to receive some free psychoanalysis, explaining a personal problem he's having with his adult son.

Caleb gives him some general psychological tips and then makes an appointment for him to come see him next week, at no charge. Grateful, Sheriff Danworth thanks Caleb, shakes his hand, climbs in his vehicle and starts the engine.

That must have been the signal for the chaos to begin. From seemingly out-of-nowhere, Sugar Bear appears and circles the car, wildly barking. Tina Weiner joins in, howling as she runs counter-clockwise to Sugar. And there, on the radio antennae is Rex, sliding down towards the windshield wipers. In one of his feet is a tiny, crumpled, dirty and yellowed paper, which he conveniently drops on the driver's side windshield.

Caleb and I both stand dumb-founded in the confusion. Sheriff Danworth gets out of the car and retrieves the paper, which I now recognize. There are only two scribbled incriminating words on that paper piece… "Becca" and "murder." Caleb seems confused, unclear as to what exactly is happening. Bolstered by my friends' unabashed courage, I race to the spot I have hidden the explosive paperwork, retrieve all pages and drop them at the sheriff's feet.

Caleb, now having a sense that something troublesome is definitely up, becomes flustered and tries to grab the pages from the sheriff's grip, but it's too late for that.

Sheriff Danworth has read enough and asks, "Just what is this all about, Caleb? This makes it look like you had something to do with the murder of your wife."

Caleb tries to reassure the sheriff that his assumptions are ridiculous, and insists that he has never seen these papers before. However, up in the top corner, is a stamp with his name and office address. The jig seems to be up and his goose seems to be cooked.

But, not yet. Caleb tries to explain the papers away by saying that Gilbertoh, as a safety precaution, had forced him to write these plots at gunpoint, so if it ever came down to it, he would be implicated in Becca's murder.

For now, Sheriff Danworth isn't buying what Caleb is selling. He reads him his rights, cuffs him and shoves him roughly into the back seat as Caleb changes his story, and pleads, "I'm telling you it was self-defense. I had no choice. She was trying to poison me."

Then I hear Caleb mutter under his breath, but just loud enough for only me to hear, "You little traitor. Son or not, you'll pay, believe me, you'll pay."

The sheriff says that he will be back for me later. I'm not stupid enough to miss his meaning… he means the pound prison. As soon as he pulls away, I don't waste any time and join my friends.

"Now what, Rex? What do I do now? I can't go back to that prison."

"You need to lay low for a while. Give me some time to think. I really have no plan in place, believing the sheriff would be so happy to collar Caleb that you would be nothing more than an afterthought. I guess I was wrong about that," laments Rex. "Why don't you hide out at Sugar Bear's until I come up with a plan to get you out safely?"

Realizing I have no alternative, I drag myself next door. I assume his parents will never notice the additional food consumption, given Sugar's OCD.

Grateful as I am, I don't like hiding out and become obsessed with self-biting. Sugar, who thinks of himself as a therapist now, offers his diagnosis that my self-biting is due to my self-loathing for my part in Becca's murder and Caleb's betrayal. Maybe he's right.

All I know for certain is that I need to have some normal distractions in my life so I head for the neighbor lady's trash in search of Rex. That's where Sheriff Danworth discovers me and contacts Animal Control.

The only saving grace is that I must be kept reasonably comfortable as I await Caleb's trial. I worry about my fate and can't help but wonder how Caleb is handling his first incarceration.

As for me, another uneventful day in the pound.

ON THE COUCH (Rex):

Hang in there, Nagi. Tea Cup, Sugar, Sideways and I are working on a plan to break you out of that prison.

ON THE COUCH (Caleb):

Another uneventful day in the county jail. Honestly, being in here is okay by me. Once Gilbertoh gets wind that he won't be receiving that insurance money, or of my attempt to implicate him in Becca's murder, he'll definitely be a little upset, may even come gunning for me. I'm safe, for now, though. After all, what harm can he possibly inflict in here?

Besides, this gives me time to build my case. All along Becca was poisoning me, so what choice did I have? It's clearly self-defense, right? Any juror with half a brain would see it my way and acquit, especially since I plan on representing myself. No one could possible do a better job laying out the facts and protecting my self-interests than me, not even McCoy from Law and Order television fame.

ON THE COUCH (Gilbertoh):

So Caleb tried to point the cops in my direction for that murder, plus he apparently won't be giving me that money he promised. Can you believe the nerve of this guy? Did he forget about that little written confession of his? Well, if he thinks he can get away with this, he's dead wrong. No matter. I want Caleb kept safe and healthy. His fate is in my hands, and mine alone. I look foward to giving him exactly what he deserves. Soon dear Caleb, soon. *Comprende?*

The End

(for now)

About the Authors

David Johnson, a licensed marriage and family therapist for more than 20 years, has an active practice in California's Central Valley. As an ex Peace Corps volunteer, David prides himself in working with all populations, inheriting his accepting attitude from his parents who he maintains were the highest examples of self-sacrifice. A pet owner his entire life, he currently parents two pound rescues, Zuli and Lobo. According to David, animals should never be underestimated in their roles in uplifting the human condition, and that they never get enough credit for all they unselfishly offer. As a therapist for humans, he believes animals are truly life's co-therapists.

Award-winning journalist Morgan Voorhis is an avid animal lover and vocal supporter of the SPCA. She has written several published stories on the benefits of having pets, proper care of these pets, and the deplorable reality of how disposable they are. As a pet parent to Zuli and Lobo, she often comments, "if humans could be as loving and consistent as animals, the world could change for the better."

9 781943 050475